About the Author

Heather Skow currently lives in Westfield, MA. She grew up in Holland, MA, and after experiencing much trauma in her own life, she was inspired to write *The Cake House*. Heather enjoys hiking, reading, coloring, writing, watching Netflix, the beach, and laughing with her husband.

The Cake House

Heather Skow

The Cake House

Olympia Publishers
London

www.olympiapublishers.com
OLYMPIA PAPERBACK EDITION

Copyright ©Heather Skow 2024

The right of Heather Skow to be identified as author of this work has been asserted in accordance with sections 77 and 78 of the Copyright, Designs and Patents Act 1988.

All Rights Reserved

No reproduction, copy or transmission of this publication may be made without written permission.
No paragraph of this publication may be reproduced, copied or transmitted save with the written permission of the publisher, or in accordance with the provisions of the Copyright Act 1956 (as amended).

Any person who commits any unauthorized act in relation to this publication may be liable to criminal prosecution and civil claims for damage.

A CIP catalogue record for this title is available from the British Library.

ISBN: 978-1-80439-842-5

This is a work of fiction.
Names, characters, places, and incidents originate from the writer's imagination. Any resemblance to actual persons, living or dead, is purely coincidental.

First Published in 2024

Olympia Publishers
Tallis House
2 Tallis Street
London
EC4Y 0AB

Printed in Great Britain

Dedication

This book is dedicated to Ash and Allisha. Mom loves you so much! And to Erik, for encouraging me to reach my potential!

Acknowledgments

I would like to thank my older child, Ash, for looking over the pages for me and letting me know of any changes I should make within the context. This novel started off as a short story I was going to submit to a contest asking to write a manuscript involving a chocolate cake. After I finished the short story, I decided to continue writing and soon I had enough words to call it a novel. I hope you enjoy reading Elise's story just as much as I enjoyed writing it.

Chapter 1

Packing my belongings into my large purple backpack gives me a feeling of solace. My breath is heavy, but I am shot with the notion that I am really ready. I believe... no, wait... I know that I am ready. I reach my arms up high while on my tiptoes, like I am thrusting my hands toward the ceiling with my shirt exposing my midriff. Then I bring them back down, gently, to my sides. I am ready to finally escape the torture, the threats, the confusion, the gaslighting, the worry, the pain, the constant heartbreak and squashed hope, and the feeling of loneliness that was my entire childhood. At seventeen years old, I'm feeling liberation, finally enduring the palpable feeling of dominance in my decision making. Twirling around my room makes me feel like Anna Pavlova on stage during her heart-throbbing performance of *Don Quixote*, the fibers of my rug swirling against my sock as the afternoon sunlight shines through my bay window, illuminating the particles of dust that spread over everything that I have owned. I raise my comforter into the air and lay it down softly onto my bed, how the birds assisted Cinderella with smoothing out her blanket on her bed in the morning. It was her help when she had work to do. Spreading out the imperfections that were sprawled out on the mattress, I make my bed one last time. As I always remember, this has been my safe space. My walls are painted spring green – the way my mom painted them when she was pregnant with me and wanted a neutral color because she was committed to having my gender be a surprise.

Posters of Nirvana, Green Day, and Madonna hang up on my walls aligning with my acrylic pour canvases. The full-size bed with an extremely comfortable bob-o-pedic mattress has been my dream catcher for as long as I am willing to remember. A cherry wood headboard sits behind it, and fairy lights hang above and down the sides with colors that match my Himalayan pink salt lamp. I have a Death Note anime comforter set, which stands out against the enchanted forest theme. I will miss this room. Shutting my eyes and throwing myself back-first onto my bed with my arms spread out wide is like dropping onto a cloud.

Turning my head toward my open closet, my eyes lock with Mr. Cat-a-corn's. Mr. Cat-a-corn is the half cat, half unicorn staring directly at me with his purple, sparkling googly eyes and protracted whiskers from the top shelf. Mr. Cat-a-corn came with me to every doctor's appointment, playdate, and bedtime ritual until I was ten. My grandma brought him to the hospital when I was born and as it turned out, it was right before she died. As I lift myself up, I wipe the strands of hair that were tickling my cheek and push them back into my messy ponytail and walk over to my fury friend. As I drag him off the shelf, a box of beads falls, splashing a colorful hue all over my rug like an exploding rainbow.

I look down and shrug. "Oh well, I guess I don't have to clean that up!" I smile devilishly at Mr. Cat-a-corn. He's so cute with his embroidered smile with his felt tongue sticking out, faded rainbow fur, and gold sequence heart on his belly. I spare him a light squeeze. He smells like coconut yogurt and cinnamon. I snuggled him even when he was covered in dirt and smooshed up animal crackers. I read him books, and he played with me and provided as much comfort as a caring parent would.

"I certainly can't keep you lying around here. You know too

many secrets! Plus, you deserve better too! You, my lifetime friend, will fit in my backpack, as long as I don't zip it up all the way." Wrapping my arms around him brings me back to a better, more attractive part of my childhood—pulling him close to my beating heart, so tight I could have popped a puppy's head off. I can see my reflection in the plastic covering his eyes. I wipe the dust off of his pupils, hoping he is ready for more adventures. This one is unpredictable, but exciting, nonetheless.

Sighing gives me relief, like exhaust steaming out from a car. It must be how a whale feels when blowing water out of its blowhole. I walk over to the kitchen and grab two out of the five credit cards my dad keeps in his junk drawer. You would think a domestic terrorist would have a safe full of cash, but not my dad. He carries a wallet full of cash and leaves the cards at home for 'emergencies.' Anyway, I think this will do for now. I hope.

This is certainly an emergency for me. After all these years, he owes me. Now I kinda wish I was darting out of here with cold hard cash. That would make this experience even more stimulatingly pleasant. For every smack in the face, every time he pulled on my hair, and I could feel the strands ripping from my skull, and he held his hand over my mouth as I tried to scream.

This whole experience reminds me of an anime called *The Promised Neverland*, but instead of a bunch of kids being trapped in an orphanage and then brought to be killed, it's just me, and there's been a way out for a while. I never felt like I could escape before because if I went to a neighbor or a friend, they would just rush me back because my dad does "such a great job taking care of me."

I head back to my room and place the cards along with a few of my picture memories from my childhood into the front pocket of my backpack and I zip it up. There's a black and white picture of my mom holding me in her arms when I was an infant, and I have a few nice pictures with Dad when he was in a cheerful mood. This was usually due to him receiving a promotion at work or bringing a woman home with him the night before who doesn't have the ability to see right through him.

I never could understand the brain capacity of these women; spending valuable time with a monster that spends his time abusing his only child. But my mom was one of those women, and she was kind-hearted. I remember her warm touch and smile. Her voice was gentle and kind, and she sang lullabies like a nightingale on a rainy morning. At least, this is how I imagine her because I am still not quite sure if this is a real memory.

Suddenly, I wake up from my deep thought as I hear the crackling sound of tires running over rocks on the gravel driveway. My heart races to my throat, and I can barely breathe. He's home early, and I planned to escape before he arrived. This can't be happening right now.

"Okay, okay, it's all right, Elise, just relax and play it cool." The sound of the tires rolling stops. "Okay, playing it cool is not as easy as it sounds."

A cold sweat breaks free from my face and neck as I hear the footsteps on the front porch and then the key turning in the lock. My hand swipes my forehead, wiping the sweat, so I can appear calm on the outside even with my panic on the inside. I've gotten good at that, but I also know now that I cannot just keep pretending like this is some aporia, I truly cannot take one more day living with this man! The door creaks open, and the keys crash like a heavy satchel full of change onto the kitchen table. The footprints are making an eerie sound and squeaking from not fully picking his shoes up against the hardwood floor. The drawer opens, and then the drawer slams shut, and it pounds through my nervous system like someone is banging on a closed door.

I pull one of my favorite Nancy Drew books out from the shelf-frame. In this book, Nancy is helping an Italian prince prove to his family that he gave a painting that belonged to the family away in good faith. I pretend I'm reading it as I sit down cross-legged on my bed. A shiver runs down my spine. I should have crawled out of the window while he was coming through the door, but it's too late now.

It takes a few minutes for him to come to my room, but he soon stumbles in, probably already had a few beers. He moves toward me, kneels down, and puts his hand on my knee. The light now illuminates the bags under his eyes and the yellow coffee stains on his teeth. He removes the book out of my hands at a leisure pace and places it down beside me. He puts his other hand on my cheek.

"Sugar plum," he says with a devious smile. "Do you happen to know why I am missing two credit cards from my drawer?"

He catches me look over to my backpack, and seconds go by, as I stare a worried glare into his eyes, and the feeling of him knowing what I am thinking is discernable. I quickly and satisfyingly lean back and kick him hard in the face and rise up. He resiliently jumps up and pulls my hair back as I'm reaching for my backpack. Although it is a challenge, I am able to struggle out of his grasp and seize my backpack.

As I run for the door of my room, he grabs my legs, and I fall face first to the floor. I feel paralyzed, glancing down at his calm and collected looking face staring back at me. He starts to pull me in by my ankles, and I'm slipping back in like I'm being swallowed by unforgiving quicksand. First, I try to squirm and pull myself forward with my hands grasping at the rug on the floor, then I grab a hold of my bookshelf and push inward as hard as I can.

The bookshelf falls on him. I kick his hands off, grab my backpack, and pick myself up. I struggle to catch my breath. I turn around in the doorway looking back into my room. Then there's a pause. My eyes looking down at his body lying on the floor, sprawled out, appearing lifeless, covered in mystery novels and a huge wooden case. He's out, but probably not for long. I book it to the front door, turn the knob, and the cool breeze smacks at my skin, sending a wave of shivers throughout my body. I'm free! As my sneakers trample off the porch, I bend down, grab a rock and toss it through the window of my dad's shiny black truck.

I keep running without looking back, and I don't stop even when I reach the main road. I keep running, watching the cars and the trees blur by until I can barely breathe. When I slow down to a stop, I lean over, and put my hands on my knees trying to catch my breath. Strands of hair are now swiping my forehead, and I can feel the sweat and oil seeping into my pores. I look up; the rays of the sun are still blinding so I squint. I form a bill with my hand to block out brightness, and right in front of me is a sign to the Days Inn hotel. I need a place to stay for now, so I enter.

Chapter 2

When I make my way through the sliding doors, I'm invited by a desk placed right in front of me. Behind the desk, there stands a stocky kid about my age, with round glasses and thick lenses. To the left, there is a set of four red leather chairs that are framed with wood on the back and on the sides with some tacky polka dot design painted on them.

There's a glass coffee table in the middle, a TV hanging on the wall, and a remote fireplace underneath. The rugs are checkered with different shades of red. To the right, there is an elevator and further down there is a long hallway with a small bar at the end. There's no one sitting at the bar, there's just a bartender polishing a shot glass with a white washcloth. I shift my eyes back to the desk in front of me.

"Hello," I say to the stocky kid who is staring at me as I do my scan of the entrance. He's wearing a pink polo shirt. My eyes find an orange tag with a white printed label. "Jacob! I need a room for... let's start with one night."

"Sure thing," he says, eyes focused on the screen and one hand on the mousepad, scrolling to find an available room.

"Ah-ha! Room 308 has just been cleaned, and it's ready for an occupant. It will be $89 for one night." He looks up at me for a couple of seconds then back at the computer screen and pauses for a moment. "We have a free complimentary breakfast in the morning..." There's another pause and I'm temporarily unresponsive. "The pool is closed for renovation." He squints at the screen. "We do have a hot tub... oh wait, that's actually closed for now also."

"Whatever, I'll take the room." Reaching into the pocket of my backpack, I pull out a paperclip and Dad's credit cards – a MasterCard and an American Express. I look at the name on the front – Jason Samson – and I shamefully glance back up, remembering that even though I ran a long way, I'm still not far from home.

I pull the hair elastic from my ponytail, sweaty from what felt like a marathon I had just run, and I fix it up again, smoothing out the loose hairs.

"Look, I'm going to need to trust you." There's a brief pause. "If a tall seemingly charming man comes in here looking for a girl and describes me, you have to tell him I'm not here."

"Hey, I can't—" Before he finishes his sentence, I cut him off, slamming both hands down on the desk.

"Listen, if he finds me, I'm going to jump out of the third-story balcony. So, unless you want me to die on your shift, no one will know that I'm here." He turns his head slightly and pastes his eyes on the window revealing a parking lot and the pavement I will fall onto if I jump. "That's right, my friend, that's where you will get a view of my body dropping like a dead hawk falling from the sky. Except I will be alive until... SPLAT!" He flinches. "I'll be lying in a pool of blood, my limbs sprawled out everywhere." He makes a disgusted look with his face. "And that's not even the worst part." He gulps. "As my spirit lifts from my lifeless body, you will be left with the **guild** and the possible fear of me haunting you in your *sleep!* You will be the one responsible for calling the paramedics and the clean-up crew. You will be questioned by people probing you for answers. They will be wondering when the last time was you spoke to me, and what did I say? And I will be watching you!"

"Okay, okay, I get it!" Jacob shouts.

"So, you understand?"

His mouth drops, eyes widen, and he nods his head up and down slowly, in both understanding and agreement.

"I'll also take one of those chicken and broccoli alfredo healthy choice meals, a Twix, and a water." I point to the display shelf behind him that has a freezer with frozen food, a refrigerator, and snacks for convenience. He brings me the items like a robot, and I walk away with the food and my check-in room card and head to the elevator.

I don't think Dad will call the police to come and find me. If he does, I'll just tell them about his hunting rifle he carries without a license. He will lose the right to see me ever again if that happens. My heart sinks. I am finally on my own, independent, and tremendously confused. *Where do I go from here?*

I reach back into my backpack and pull out Mr. Cat-a-corn, giving him a nervous squeeze as the doors to the elevator close me in. On the way up, I unwrap my candy and stuff my face with the caramel shortbread chocolate bar for comfort. I didn't think it would also hurt a bit... to run away, planning to never look back again, but it does.

Maybe I need to speak with a therapist. I can already feel the weight of the trauma bond. Mrs. Avery, my second-grade teacher, suggested my dad get a therapist because I didn't have a mother figure in the home. He politely declined and told her it was nonessential. As if he knew what it was like to live without a mother. His mother was my only living grandmother, and she treated him like a little prince. She didn't believe her son was capable of doing anything wrong. She was the only one who saw him abusing me, and she didn't care. She would take me out for ice cream like nothing had happened. I guess what they say is true, the apple doesn't fall far from the tree.

Taking it easy for the rest of the evening is exactly what I needed. I take a long, steamy shower, slip into my *Cinderella* pajamas, and then I plop down on the king-sized bed. The quilt and sheets are nice and snug. The room is a warm temperature, delivering a peaceful atmosphere, perfect for the day I had.

I flip through the television until I find *an I Dream of Jeannie* marathon. I begin to feel comfortable as vague memories of seeing and hearing these characters cross my mind. I don't remember Dad ever watching this show, and it's pretty good. I watch, with my arms around Mr. Cat-a-corn, until my eyes grow heavy, and I drift into a deep sleep.

When I open my eyes and turn to look at the alarm clock sitting on the nightstand, it reads 1:23 a.m. I turn away and glance at the ceiling, letting out an exhale of uncertainty. I notice some dark shadow pasted on the ceiling. Squinting, the left side of my nose arches. I move myself to get a closer look. I'm confused because I'm the only one in this room. Well, I'm supposed to be the only one in this room.

Sitting up straight and slowly turning my neck again to the left, a wave of cool air brushes up against my skin, and it feels like it's hovering over me.

I quickly raise the sheets up over my head and struggle to steady my pulse. I feel the cool air again press against the sheets, giving a heavy, unsettling feeling like wet cement is pouring over me. I lift the sheets off my head and look back to the left.

There's a shadow of a human walking out of the bathroom! I squint again, and glare at this preposterous being interrupting my slumber and probably here to tear my guts out! It literally just looks like a 3D shadow. Almost like a human in a black fitted body cover.

"What the heck?" I whisper to myself.

The shadow grows larger, and its color begins to change. It's more yellowish now, transforming into something massive. It's a sea lamprey! I have never seen one in person before. I read in this book one time that they suck the blood and other fluids out of their prey! This is petrifying, nerve-wrenching, spine-chilling even.

The sea creature inches its way over to my bed at a rapid speed and opens its enormous circular mouth filled with hundreds of razor-sharp teeth.

This sea lamprey is both invasive and unbidden. Watching it closely, I start to see a person climbing up out of the throat, stand up, and reach his right hand out for me to grab. I blink a few times before it becomes evident that this person is Dad! His eyes are wild and ghostly. His hand is just a foot away from me, and I have no intention of reaching back out to him. My face fills with disgust. I shake my head "no." I close my eyes, wanting for the ocean brute to leave with my dad.

Suddenly, the alarm clock goes off. I open my eyes. It is six a.m. I rise and try to catch my breath. I swallow the lump in my throat and find myself thanking God in my head that it was only a dream. My arms reach out over my head to stretch as I yawn. Then I slip on some jeans, draw a t-shirt over my head, and throw my hair into a ponytail.

It's early in the morning. I peek into the bathroom to be sure there's no shadow lurking around, and I brush my teeth. I'm up early enough to go enjoy some free breakfast. So, I head to the elevator and back down to the dining area to stuff my face with some food.

Chapter 3

As I sit alone eating my scrambled eggs and bagel, a flock of pigeons gather outside of the window beside me, scurrying around because there is a threatening hawk roaming right above them. I swipe the remains of my eggs around the plate to add some unconscious rhythm to my boredom. My attention wanders, and I overhear a small group of friends, about my age, gossiping about J.K. Rowling and talking about how they are heading to Westfield, Massachusetts.

"She was rich before she became an author. She had everything handed to her," the pretty boy says.

"Nah, she was poor, and *Harry Potter* made her affluent," one girl protests. "She was actually on welfare, writing *Harry Potter* from a coffee shop. I saw it on some show, but I don't remember which one."

"Whatever, why are we even talking about this? Have you secured our spot at the campground, Allison?"

It's a quad of two males and two females who probably planned some little double date getaway that I'm about to invite myself into as a fifth wheel. I know I need to leave this town, find a job, and another place to stay, so I justify my little intrusion by confirming to myself that this is my one ticket out. At the coffee station, I notice a small shelf with brochures and maps. I grab a map before I sit back down, still eavesdropping on their conversation with every movement.

Westfield is about 130 miles from here, and I really don't

care where I'm going as long as it's not here. After listening for a few more minutes, I find out by the dude in dreads that they will be gassing up their van and heading out soon. So now I know they may have enough room for me. The typical van holds about four people in the back and two in the front two seats. As they get up to throw away their trash, I get up, speed up ahead of them and turn around with my hands up in front of me – gesturing them to come to a stop.

"Um, hey, I hear you are heading to Westfield. I am heading that way myself, except I don't have a car. Can I ride with you?"

I'm heading 130 miles away, but I don't have a car? They must think I'm crazy. I feel my face flush and my hands clam up because I am shy about asking for favors. Probably because Dad never liked when I expressed what I wanted if it was inconvenient for him. So that's what it is. I don't like to inconvenience anyone.

The four of them pause, looking me up and down. *They definitely think I'm crazy.* The tall girl with a top knot bun and large hoop earrings gives a side glance to her friends. Raising one brow, she looks back at me.

"We don't have any room for—"

Before she can finish, her friend with long blonde hair, hazel eyes, and a gold ring pierced on the side of her nose interrupts.

"Sure, we will give you a ride," she says, and the girl who rejected me gives her an adverse reaction, then pulls a tootsie roll pop out of her Coach purse and removes the wrapper. She presses it against her glossy lips. I am going to guess that it is strawberry-kiwi-flavored lip gloss. My nostrils pick up the scent as if I had just smeared it on my own dry, dehydrated lips.

"It's my van, and I like helping people, so she can come with us." She looks back at me. "My name is Allison, and this is

Chloe, Tyler, and James."

The two boys give a wave. Chloe stands there, with her tootsie roll pop, rolling her eyes. She stands up tall, and her shirt lifts, exposing her midriff. Her bracelets are dangling, a mixture of semi-precious beads and sterling silver. She crosses her arms.

"I'm Elise and thank you so much for letting me come with you." I almost want to give Allison a hug, but instead decide that that may be going a bit overboard.

"It's no problem." Allison gives a warm, genuine smile.

After disposing our trash, we all head out into the large, white minivan full of heavy metal stickers, removing any attention that may be drawn to the many dents in the rear, that may have been the result of backing up hastily after one too many drinks at a social gathering.

The ride is a little cramped, and my nerves rack every time we have to stop and allow "Duchess" (that's the name Allison gave to the van) to take a breather. A couple of times we had to open the hood and let the smoke air out. On both occasions, I felt as if it may be safer if I stop in any town, at any hotel with surroundings full of buildings, businesses, and construction. Not just mountains and trees. I'd rather not end up a dinner party for some wolves or black bears. I'd rather not be trampled on by a 1200-pound moose.

In between each of the anxiety-filling stops, we listen to a collection of different music genres ranging from Gangster Rap to Jamaican Reggae. There doesn't seem to be anything that this clan does not listen to for music. It is entertaining. I keep myself distracted by searching for yellow cars. This was the one thing Dad did that made long rides to places more enjoyable. We would play games like 'I Spy' or he would ask me to count how many yellow cars I can spot on the way to our destination. Thinking about this hurts me because I wish that Dad wasn't so volatile, that there were more positive moments that I shared with him.

When we arrive in Westfield, I hop out of the vehicle at a gas station, and I'm reeking of marijuana and New Ports. Allison asks if I would like to stay with them at a campground. I decide to depart from the group here and walk around town looking for a job. Possibly settling down in another hotel with a local newspaper to find someone looking for a roommate or something will be a useful deposit of my time.

Westfield is a nice town with many restaurants and stores. I spot some Vietnamese cuisine, Mexican, Puerto Rican, Japanese, and Thai. There are trees that line the sidewalks with clear mini lights wrapped around them. It must look pretty at night. Walking along the sidewalk, I spot a bakery called The Cake House with a "Now Hiring" sign on the front door.

In the window, there are all different types of cakes and other desserts. I notice a triple layer chocolate cake with layers of dark chocolate, and it's decorated with chocolate butter cream, drizzled with more chocolate running down the edges, and topped with chocolate truffles. My mouth is watering at the sight, and I would love to sit down and stuff my face with just about any one of these sugary sweets right now.

I remember that I need to work more than I need to indulge in tasty treats right now. I walk into a room with a glass shelf holding even more nicely decorated treats along the right side. Next to the cash register, there is a giant book of wedding cakes. On the left side, there are small circular café tables with chairs, and vases of daisies rest in the middle of each one. I'm taken away by the scent of chocolate and vanilla and freshly baked pastries.

The walls are a vibrant sapphire yellow dressed in awards

from various baking competitions and pictures of a red-haired woman next to… no surprise… more cake! There's no one at the register so I flip through the wedding cake book for a few minutes.

Suddenly, a middle-aged woman walks out from a door in the corner. She is an attractive female with shoulder-length red hair, emerald green eyes, and a tiny nose. She's wearing crimson red lipstick that matches the blush smeared on her high cheekbones. She's dressed in a green and white checkered apron over a black short-sleeved camisole dress that hangs down to her knees. She's pretty toned. She must do yoga or palates in her free time.

"Are you here to place an order?" she asks as I hurry to close the book and place it back on the counter.

"I'm actually here because of your sign in the window. The one that says you are hiring."

"Oh good, the help quit yesterday so you can start right away. My name is Claire, and you are…?"

"Elise, but I do have to tell you that I don't have much work experience. I really have no good references. I actually just ran away from my dad's house and basically hitchhiked here from Portsmouth, New Hampshire. I also need a place to stay because I don't want him to find me, and I just can't go back. He's hurt me too many times." Tears begin to flow rapidly from my eyes, and this is the first time since I left that I became so vulnerable, and it all came out at once.

Claire blinks as she absorbs everything, I have just told her. Her eyes gloss up, and they're filled with authenticity and concern. Her arms open wide as she walks over and wraps them around me.

"You poor dear, I also have a vacant studio in the loft upstairs. I live right across the street, but you can stay in the room here. A young woman like you deserves to have some privacy. You can stay upstairs as long as you need to, and you can work for me here."

"Thank you so much!" A sudden feeling of relief flows through me like a gentle stream. Claire already seems so nice, and I appreciate that she is offering me a job and a place to stay! I didn't expect something like this to happen so fast.

My pulse quickens at the thought that this could be too good to be true, but I remember my background and everything I have been through. Not everyone is going to be looking to take advantage of me.

My mind shifts back to the excitement of the generous offer. I am going to be the best employee she has ever had! Regardfully, she guides me upstairs to where I will be staying. It is a small room with a roof-shaped ceiling. There's a bed up against the wall, a bathroom, one closet, and a tiny kitchen area. A large window reveals a beautiful backyard full of trees and rose bushes.

"It's not much, but feel free to make it your own."

"No, this is perfect!"

It is more than I would have asked for entering a new town and meeting the first friendly woman in it. I hug her and squeeze her so tight. I have never connected with another woman through a tight embrace like this before. It feels warm and comforting, the way I imagined it would be with my own mother.

Chapter 4

Weeks pass, and I find that working with Claire hasn't really felt like work at all. I spend workdays at the cash register, taking orders from people who are planning parties, weddings, and birthdays. It feels like I'm an essential part of the community. It fills me with joy to help people make the best of these important days of their lives.

I got to help a little girl with beautiful red mermaid hair decide on a Hawaiian-themed birthday party with a yellow cake, smeared in vanilla frosting, colored with ocean blue dye, creating waves against the graham cracker crumb sand. I helped a bride pick out the perfect cake in the shape of a castle with witch-hat towers and rose vine candies wrapped around them.

Claire helped me set up a TV with cable and Internet in my room, and I get a paycheck on Fridays, so I buy some new decorations and art supplies. I got some new lights and a large pink Himalayan salt lamp, taller than the one I had in my old room. I found someone at the farmer's market who paints pictures of rock stars, so I got her to paint a picture of Billy Joe Armstrong – the lead singer of Green Day – on a canvas for me. Painting reminds me of home, and I feel a needle-like pain through my heart when I think of redecorating with art.

Dad would make art projects with me, and I don't know why I'm filled up with emptiness and the aching feeling throbs through my veins thinking about it. I find it therapeutic at the same time. Free time extends itself, so I make a cat with large orange sunglasses smoking a cigar with a fire-like sunset behind him and a dragon breathing out rainbow flames for my wall.

"Would you like meatloaf for dinner?" Claire shouts from the bottom step.

I run down the stairs because I'm hungry after all of this work, and I also love meatloaf.

"Come on over to my place, and I will fix you a plate."

We both walk over to Claire's house together, and when we get through the doors, Damien greets us with a feisty meow, then rolls over on his back for a belly scratch. Damien is Claire's best friend - a cat, and he's a friendly mixture of white and black with a brown spot over his left eye. I playfully scratch his fat belly and he maliciously scratches at my wrists and runs away.

Washing the wounds in the kitchen reminds me of when I would scrape my knees on the pavement when I would ride my bike as a young child. Claire hands me some band aids, and it is as if I have covered not just one open wound.

"He means no harm, he's just weary of new guests," she says.

I shake my head after she turns away from me, and we both sit down to eat. The meatloaf looks delectable, and there's a side of buttery mashed sweet potatoes with a hint of cinnamon and green beans smothered in olive oil and chopped-up garlic. There's just a touch of lemon juice to play with my taste buds.

"I was working full time at a bakery when I was your age as well," she continues, "I also had to leave an abusive home. My father was a corrections officer who used to lock me in the cellar when I did something wrong. My mom was an angry alcoholic who slept with multiple people during their dysfunctional marriage. Anyhow, she was very... let's say... unsure of her sexuality. She would sleep with men and women. It didn't matter who, or what their intentions were.

"It was because of all my hard work I was able to soon start up my own business." She takes a bite of her meatloaf and a sip of her wine. I take a bite of my meatloaf. It is perfectly moist with a hint of some tangy-flavored sauce. *Something with onions and just a touch of mango?* I swallow. I have nothing to drink so I excuse myself by grabbing a glass of water with ice cubes.

"Do you think someday I could own a successful business?" I continue while I'm pouring water over the ice in my glass.

"I think you surely have the talent; it depends on whether you are committed to the hard work and challenges." She takes another sip of wine. As I sit back down, I look over at the bottle, and it's almost finished. I bite down into my savory meatloaf, and I wonder if Claire is truly happy with the way her life turned out. I'm also wondering why I'm tasting some orange flavor with Worcestershire sauce.

We finish our meals with a little less conversation, and I do the dishes then head back over to my room to fix it up and make it pretty.

On Wednesday, Claire and I order takeout, and she teaches me how to bake in the kitchen while we sing along to Fleetwood Mac songs that we blast so loud and could care less who hears us. I feel like she is the mom I didn't get to have. My real mom died when I was three so my best memories of her are jumping on my bed while she shoots bubbles out of a bubble gun and singing "Baby Beluga."

Claire lives alone with Damien. I have been coming over to her house more often, and we watch horror movies, or I show her some anime that I like. She seems to have very few friends in her life, just people she knows from baking competitions, and Larry, the janitor. She doesn't talk much about her family, except for when she opened up about abuse. We have a lot in common in that area. She's a cool lady who enjoys having me around.

The sun sets as I walk back to my room after having apricot chicken, rosemary broccoli, and buttery mashed potatoes with sour cream and gravy, and a Mediterranean salad at Claire's. It leaves the sky with a hint of orange and pink. The streetlights reflect off tiny puddles on the concrete and leave halos on the hoods of vehicles parked near the sidewalk.

When I walk inside, I get this urge to make a chocolate cake by myself. Not just any chocolate cake, one with layers, decorations, and candy on top! Usually, Claire stacks the layers when we make them together, but I've been feeling inspired by her talents lately, and I want to show her a cake that I mixed up from scratch and put together on my own. I not only want to see the look on her face, but I also want to see for myself if I can do it.

Of course, I love chocolate, so I browse through Claire's recipes and find a peanut butter chocolate layer cake. Right above the directions and ingredients, there's a picture of a slice with three layers of chocolate cake. In between the layers and covering on the outside of the cake, there is creamy peanut butter frosting. My eyes are already in dessert heaven.

There are chopped pieces of Reese's peanut butter cups on top and between the layers! Ganache is drizzled on the sides. I can feel my mouth salivating. This cake is going to be delicious. The pastry Chef who wrote the cookbook says she loves making this cake for her book clubs and as a dessert for a mid-week dinner with the family. She bakes to have something creative to focus on when life gets chaotic.

I gather all the ingredients and begin mixing the wet ingredients and then adding the dry ingredients. I can already smell the peanut butter, chocolatey sweetness as it swirls around in the KitchenAid. When I remove the cake pans from the oven, I start mixing the peanut butter frosting and the ganache, and then I chop the Reese's.

Sometimes, Claire refrigerates the cake for an hour before layering the frosting, but I am impatient, and I want to complete it tonight. I'm just too energized and filled with excitement.

As I frost one layer of the cake and add the next layer, it begins to fall apart a little, but I made enough frosting to cover it up. By the time I add the third layer, one of the sides caves in, and as I try to even it out with more frosting, some sides start to crack. It looks like a chocolate earthquake! I feel tired at this point so I add the ganache because maybe that will help cover up some of the cracks. I add the chopped Reese's and decorate with more icing using a piping bag.

There are still so many dents and cracks. "Oh well, that doesn't mean it won't be absolutely flavorful." When I finish, I'm surprisingly not that hungry. Well, I have been eating some of the Reese's and frosting during the making of this project. I decide it will make a great breakfast. I place my lovely, cracked cake into a cake stand, cover it up, and head upstairs to bed.

Another strange dream makes its way into my brain that night. This time something creeps up the stairs. I swallow the lump in my throat as I hear each stair creek. When the eerie creature cracks the door open, it first reveals a collection of black furry legs hugging the edge of the door. Then it pulls itself into my room to further reveal its ghastly figure. It is all black against the darkness, so it is difficult to make out. Squinting is what I resort to as a solution, but that still doesn't help until the being steps onto a trail of light falling onto the room from the streetlamp outside my window. It is then confirmed to be a giant goliath bird-eating spider. The scary spider creeps over to face me at a similar pace as it did while making its way up the staircase. We fall into a deep staring contest, with my sheets and comforter held up over my mouth and nose, until it gives up and scurries out of my room and back down the steps.

There was no Dad, no burning or blinding, or whatever it is goliath bird-eating spiders do to their prey. I'm thankful again when I'm awakened by the loud beeping of my alarm clock. I lift myself up out of bed, gather my thoughts (well, do my best to process these thoughts). What could be the meaning of these dreams? Maybe I should pick up a book about dreams from that used bookstore with a blue umbrella over the sign I saw one day walking around town, Blue Umbrella Books it is called. *Maybe there's one at the local library?* I shake it off and imitate a few light yoga poses that I've seen on TV, and then after that I put on my work clothes. I can't quite shake this anxious throb in my chest, wondering if maybe the internet will have some answers about the imagery in these dreams. A deep breath darts its way through my respiratory system, inflating my stomach and then making a dent in it like a release of air through a paper bag as I head down the stairs. Slowly I stumble. I'm lightheaded and feel a bit nauseous.

Maybe eating a sugary breakfast will help because it could be low blood sugar after all. I work my way back upstairs, holding on tight to the railing and pulling myself up. With blurred vision and a fuzzy mind, I make myself a bowl of fruit loops. *What is it about this dream that has me feeling so... off?*

I almost want to take the day off from work, but I remember

what Claire said about hard work paying off. I must work through this!

I think you surely have the talent; it depends on whether you are committed to the hard work and challenges.

When I regain energy and feel less nauseated, I go back downstairs to work. Claire's probably right, it's important to put your work ahead of everything else.

When I finally arrive downstairs, work starts off busy and continues that way through the entire morning. Tons of locals picking up desserts. At noon, right before I am about to have my lunch, a fortunate-looking boy comes in to pick up a cake for his little brother's birthday party. It's a funfetti cake with a unicorn in the middle. The boy looks like he's a couple of years older than me. He has peacock blue eyes and messy sienna brown hair. He has a straight nose and a goatee. He's wearing a navy-blue polo shirt and blue jeans that are lightly faded with small rips on the thigh and knees, and they look like they came straight off the mannequin in the display window at Hollister. They hang low on his hips.

"What a babe!" I accidentally blurt out in a casual tone. "Um what I meant to say… what a great cake design choice!"

He looks like he's amused and interested. His attentive look and posture convey the idea that he would like to be more involved.

I take the pick-up receipt he's been holding out for me. I notice that his pupils enlarge a little, and his cheeks are rosy. He stands there for a little while with the box in his hands. It is as if he is looking for something else to say, but he just can't find the words. His eyes widen as if he just found the solution to global warming.

"Oh, can I also try a piece of that cake behind you?" he says, pointing to the shelf behind me.

Turning around I realize that I had placed my Reese's chocolate cake on that shelf. My eyes close for a second in embarrassment. No one was supposed to see that. *He wants a piece of my demented cake? Does he need to see an optometrist?* There are perfectly decorated cakes right in front of his face. *Oh boy, I hope it at least tastes good. I haven't tried it yet. Now I remember what my breakfast plans were.*

"Um... sure," I hesitate for a moment. *Can I even say no?*

I try to let go of my low self-esteem, and I cut him a slice of the cake and place it into a small box. I giggle as I hand him the box, and I feel blood rushing to my cheeks.

"My name is Jared," he states. I didn't ask for his name, but I guess I'm compelled to tell him mine.

"Elise!" I hear Claire yell as she walks out of the kitchen, and she seems furious. My heart tightens.

"You didn't finish cleaning the bathroom like I asked you to!"

I thought that was Larry's job, and I don't remember her asking me to do that, but she's really upset, and I have never seen her angry at me before. Her face is as red as a tomato. She places her hands on her hips, demanding an explanation.

"I'll take over here, and you go back there and finish what I asked you to do." She points to the corner door.

Embarrassed by Claire's interruption, I hurriedly walk out of the room and into the bathroom. I close the bathroom door and press my back against it. It doesn't even look that dirty. I'm trying to understand what just happened. *Why did she interrupt a conversation I was having? With such a dreamy guy I may never have the chance to talk to him again, and he asked for a slice of my cake.* At this point, I am frustrated. *But maybe Claire is just having a bad day. Maybe if I clean this bathroom like she asks, we can forget I ever got her this mad.*

As I am down on my knees, with rubber gloves on, scrubbing the floor, Claire's furious tomato face crosses my mind again. I don't believe it; I made her furious by having an extra five-minute conversation with a boy that ordered a birthday cake? I've had plenty of other conversations with customers. I shake my head and breathe out heavily. I feel my nostrils flair out. Then I try my hardest to brush off the unpleasant encounter and gather supplies to clean the bathroom top to bottom.

Finishing the cleaning job brings me relief, and I bring the mop, the sponges, and the bleach cleaner back to the closet. My nausea returns along with my brain fuzziness. It must be the low blood sugar again. I march back upstairs to my room so that Claire doesn't see me not working. I'm taking a break. I cut myself a large slice of cake. The cake that I made all by myself.

My palms are sweaty as I pull myself up to eat it, one hand on the railing, another on my ceramic plate with a slice of cake on it. When I reach my studio and shovel a piece into my mouth, I close my eyes as I am taken away to a French restaurant beside the river across from the Eiffel Tower in Paris. Dozens of colorful butterflies' float around me as they flap their wings around the pink and white rose vines. Suddenly, a marble falls from the counter, and I awaken from my short vacation. When I finish with my dessert, I realize that I need some protein. There are some left-over meatloaf and potatoes in my refrigerator. That does it. I finish it all and leave the plate and Tupperware in the sink. It is easy to fall asleep after I finish and take a hot shower. This has been a confusing day, and I'm glad it's over. I'm still puzzled about what could have gotten into Claire.

Chapter 5

When Wednesday rolls around, Claire and I continue to partake in our weekly delivery, baking, and singing plans. She even allowed me to have a glass of red wine!

"In Italy, wine is served for all dinner guests of all ages," she explains, waving her hand in the air like she's a spokesmodel and what she has to say is truly life changing. I wonder if I should ask if they put wine in sippy cups. I resist the urge for a sarcastic remark, and I just go with it.

"Are you Italian?" I ask. She places her index and middle finger to her chin as if she's pondering. Then she changes the subject.

"Do you know that you can replace butter with avocados in baking if you are on a diet?" I shift my lips to the side, as if I want to kiss my own cheek.

"No, Claire, I didn't know that" I say softly.

She doesn't mention anything about Jared and neither do I. Although I have his beautiful smile and gorgeous eyes that melt me from the inside out on my mind. I guess her absence of boy talk is the most important take from this conversation. She seems to be fine again!

"You would look just marvelous in purple lipstick." Claire presumes randomly. She just blurts things out like it's the perfect new topic for conversation.

"Uh, thanks. You would also look good in purple lipstick." I reply and shrug my shoulders innocently. I assume it's the right thing to say.

"Oh, and have you ever thought of getting highlights?" She asks. I twirl my fingers around the dead ends of my hair, bringing them up to my eyesight. This is Claire insisting that I need a makeover and my au natural look just isn't cutting it. I just laugh nervously, and we move on from the topic.

We laugh and enjoy our night as we usually do. There are no issues that have arrived, and I'm feeling a bit tipsy from the wine. Maybe the problem was just the bathroom. I really don't remember her asking me to clean it though.

I keep hoping that I run into Jared. I mean, the only places I really go are upstairs to my studio, The Cake House, Claire's house, and sometimes the mall and grocery store… with Claire. Maybe I need more of a social life… with other people… around my age. I dropped out of school when I ran away, and I have been thinking about getting my G.E.D., but Claire keeps me busy at The Cake House, and I have everything I need. I kept a flyer someone was handing out outside of a Church advertising a book club. Am I really so desperate for belonging that I'm almost willing to read books about a religion that I know nothing about? I'll come back to that thought when I am ready, I suppose.

The line is almost out the door at The Cake House, and I notice Jared as it dwindles down. He's standing in line casually in a baseball cap, a white t-shirt, and flip flops. I'm nervous, but I wonder if he is here because he likes me. I hope my hair looks all right. I threw it up in a bun this morning. And well… he could just be getting another cake. I hope Claire doesn't catch us talking though. I won't be able to stop blushing, and she will notice, so I must keep my cool.

When he reaches the register, he coughs to clear his throat, and then he asks for a raspberry cheesecake brownie for himself and a slice of cookie dough cake. He eyeballs the pistachio cake but settles on just the two orders.

"The slice of cake is for later," he explains.

"That's cool." There's an awkward silence, and he's reluctant to leave. There's an older couple behind him and a woman in a suit who looks like she's on a mission behind them, so he has to either leave or say what he really wants to say... or maybe what I really want him to say.

"Hey, would you like to come to a party with me this weekend... Friday night? My friend from college is having a bunch of people over his parents' house. They will be out of town so it could get pretty wild." I smirk. "They have a pool, a Jacuzzi, and a full bar. Some of my other friends are in a band, and they will be playing at his house that night." His vocal advertisement had me inclined to say 'Yes' at the word party.

I'm frozen. Not only did Jared come in to order something for himself, but he just invited me to a party. *Oh my God, he's in college? This is crazy! He has friends, and he wants me to come hang out with those friends?*

"I know it seems weird because we barely know each other, but you look like you are new in town and could use a night out."

I certainly am new in town, and I could definitely use a night out.

"I would love to!" I say in a tone that makes my desperation for human interaction a little too obvious.

"Okay, great." He laughs, reaches over to grab a pen from my pen holder, and writes his phone number down on a napkin. "Call me whenever, the party starts at eight p.m., and I can pick you up."

"Great, that sounds great." I let out a giggle. "I live here.

Well, right upstairs, so it should be no problem finding me." I give him an ear-to-ear grin and wave excitedly. I feel an overwhelming amount of hyperactivity, and it's like my heart is going to pound out of my chest and fly away!

Our conversation ends with no interruption from Claire, and he walks out the door with his cheesecake brownie and slice of cookie dough cake. I gave him a large slice. Maybe Claire didn't notice. Maybe she doesn't mind any more. Maybe she was just having a bad day the other day, and I don't have to worry about her getting mad at me for meeting a new friend.

I lean over the counter with my fist holding my chin up. I watch Jared walk to his car, and I picture us kissing up against it under a moonlit sky. The rest of the line just stands there as I gaze out the window. Suddenly, Claire does interrupt my daydream and hands me some sanitizing wipes for the counter. She smiles though and winks at me. I think things are going to be all right.

"I'll take these customers, if you will just be a dear and wipe down those tables for me."

"Yeah, no problem." Grabbing the wipes, I swipe my hair behind my ears and clean the crumbs off the tables, imagining that I'm on a magic carpet ride with my handsome Jared! I stop and notice that I've just pushed the crumbs onto the floor and grab the broom to sweep up my mess. I dance around with the broom, imagining that we have landed, and we are at my prom with dancing lights bouncing off the walls and music so loud we can't hear each other talk. The people standing in line disappear in my imagination but resurface when brought back to reality. They just stare, whispering their reactions to each other. I don't care anyway. Dream land is the place for me when an intensively attractive male just asked me out.

My party date with Jared is just hours away. Claire has been fine, though a little distant. I told her that I will be going to a party with a guy I met in the store, and it didn't seem to bother her at first.

"So, let me tell you what I know about men. If you don't give them what they want, they will leave you feeling abandoned and worthless." Claire pours herself a glass of wine and begins to gulp it. I am starting to think she's had bad experiences with men. She refills her glass, grabs another glass, and pours wine into it, placing the glass in front of me.

I am taken aback by this statement. *What could have happened to Claire?* Claire has never mentioned anything about the men in her life. I pull out a stool from her kitchen island and listen.

"I was married once."

"Wow, I had no idea you were married," I say, wondering if I want to know what happened to that marriage, but I'm also sympathetic to her drunken sore spot.

"We tried to have a baby. We tried for years to have a baby. Upstairs, I still have a nursery room. It took three miscarriages for him to file for a divorce and give up on me altogether."

Claire begins to cry, and I part myself from the kitchen island and walk around to give her a hug.

"I don't know what to say, Claire."

"No man is worth your time, darling. You deserve to build a life doing what you love. Men will only get in the way of that. Kids aren't that great either. I decided to become a nanny before I became the owner of The Cake House. Those little brats gave me migraines and enough germs for constant congestion."

"I'm sorry that all of this happened to you," I say in my most sincere voice.

Claire could be right about men. I mean, I could just keep things platonic with Jared. Claire did have everything she wanted. Her kitchen alone was beautiful with copper pots and pans that hang above her marble kitchen island. She has her stand-alone KitchenAid mixer and ultramarine blue cabinets. And then there is… of course… her flourishing business. Claire lifts her head up.

"I hope this boy you want to see treats you right. I really do. I'm so happy you are going to a party to meet new friends."

She pats me on the back and wipes the bags under her eyes with her fist. Her face is clear of make-up. She takes one last sip of wine and begins to walk sloppily to her bedroom. I follow in case she needs help. She slips on a sock in the hallway, and I catch her before she falls backward and lands on her butt. Then I help her into bed.

"Claire, my illusion of love has been shattered my whole life," I say, tucking her in. "I am just hoping to establish some friendships with people around my age."

Claire is already asleep and snoring. I watch her, peacefully in a drunken coma. I turn away to shut the lights off and leave the room. There has to be more to happiness than what Claire has. There just has to be. Claire doesn't seem that happy at all. She said her mother was an angry drunk, and she's just a sloppy drunk.

In the midst of boredom, I take a cab to the mall to get some clothes to wear to the party. I buy a low-cut tank top and a miniskirt for the occasion. No, I'm not trying to persuade attention from Jared. The sales associate helped me pick it out. She also helped me find the perfect bikini to take a dip in the pool.

I head on over to the bank to be sure my account is still healthy, and I discover that Claire has not deposited last week's pay into my account. It's always there by Friday. There must be a mistake. I brush it off for now because my main focus is on the party tonight. I am a pretty good saver. Maybe there was some delay in depositing or some interruption. I don't want to be bothered by stress right now. I'm going to a party, and parties are supposed to be fun!

After my errands, I head off to my room. I call Jared from the cordless phone that's probably been sitting in this room for a decade. When I found it, I had to brush off layers of dust. Luckily for me, it still works. Jared confirms that he will be here around seven thirty a.m. and that he can't wait to see me. I can't wait either!

I watch a YouTube video on how to successfully paint on a "Smokey eye." I use some dark blue and some gray. I apply the rest of my makeup and curl the ends of my long cocoa brown hair. I stare for a moment into my aqua blue, almond-shaped eyes. Suddenly, I'm saddened by the fact that Claire isn't helping me get ready to go out with friends. I'm going to meet new people, but right now I'm alone again.

I've always been okay on my own, but Claire made me feel like I didn't have to do things on my own any more, and now it's like she's mad at me for wanting something just as much as I want her support.

I get lost in thought for a moment until there's a knock on my bedroom door. Oh my God, it's Jared. I didn't realize it was so close to the time to leave. I race to the door and fix my skirt a little. Then I check my cleavage, and I smell my underarm. It wouldn't hurt to add a little more deodorant. I refrain from turning the doorknob for a moment to glide some on, then I tip-toe back over as if I'm sneaking around. I do one last pull of the skirt to straighten it out and check my chest again. I open the door, and he's standing at the door with a handful of handpicked sunflowers. He's dressed like a Hollister model, and his hair is still messy like it was styled by beach waves. His smile is easy and his eyes innocent.

I welcome him inside and offer him a Heineken from the stash I stole from Claire's cooler downstairs. I light a Georgia peach-scented candle and put the flowers in a cup of water since I don't own any vases. We both drink our beer and hang out in my room for a little while, talking about how glad we are it's the weekend, and he tells me how killer the party is going to be. He also assures me that I will like his friends.

I don't know how you can know that from two meetings, but I believe him. He glances over at my cherry wood entertainment center and steps toward it.

"Are these all six seasons of *My Hero Academia*? I love anime!" He explores my collection.

"You got me, I'm a sucker for anime." I blush. He continues to finger through the DVD case.

"So, what brought you to Westfield anyway?" he asks, and it seems like he has some more questions to ask about my life up his sleeve that I certainly do not want to answer right now.

"My aunt owns The Cake House, and I figured I would help her out as I save up, and she lets me stay up here… but we should get going," I say, bouncing up from my seat on my bed and gulping the last of my Heineken. I don't want to get into the fact that I'm a runaway from my abusive dad, and I really don't have any family right now. A quick change of subject usually gets me out of emotional small talk that consists of me bringing up painful memories. I don't have a normal life where I can just laugh about carelessly with others.

He sucks down the last of his beer, and we head out down the spiral stairwell that leads to my studio in the attic.

"That's my red Honda Civic over there," he yells as he hurries to catch up with me. He opens the passenger side door and lights a cigarette to take a few drags before driving off.

When we get to the party, the band is already playing Metallica which is pretty cool. People are just starting to show up and Jared brings me over to meet his friend.

"Jared, my man!" A boy dressed like him and Jared have the same closet with blond hair shaved on one side maneuvers through the crowd to get to us.

"Brian this is Elise, Elise... Brian. Brian's parents own the house."

"Yes! Welcome to my humble abode!" he yells.

Jared hands me a Lime Arita, and I start gulping that. Social interactions aren't really my thing even though it's oddly something I crave.

"This is a really nice house," I say as Brian leads us onto a semi-circular terrace where we can see the in-ground pool with a waterfall and tiny lanterns that light up the white picket fence surrounding it.

"Thank you! My parents are away in South Africa conducting research on familial emotional support and the grades of students in high school! So, I have this baby all to myself for three weeks!"

"That's awesome! So, what do they do to help these students if they don't get any emotional support from their families?"

"I don't really know! They don't talk about their work much with me! They're just out there doing what they love, and I'm over here doing what I love! Party! Woo!"

Jared grabs my hand and guides me over to introduce me to more of his friends outside. I notice the Jacuzzi off to the corner, the steam floating up in the air. I sit down at the bar with a couple of his friends who introduce themselves as Kayla and Holly. Holly is tall with long, dark hair, and Kayla is an Asian girl who has her hair tied back in two Princess Leia buns. Both girls are pretty, and I notice as they bring their cups to their lips that they have summer-inspired manicured nails.

Note to self – pick up some tropical blues and pinks for my nails. The two girls start talking about cute guys they share college classes with and life at their internships. I feel a bit awkward because I'm a high school dropout, and I don't even know if I'll ever have a normal life like them, but I am enjoying the atmosphere.

"Elise, do you have an internship yet?" Kayla asks. There's a short delay until I think of something quick.

"Uh, yeah I'm doing a culinary internship out here at a bakery for a few months. I go to school in New Hampshire."

"Oh nice, Southern New Hampshire University? My cousin goes there, you might know him. He's also in the culinary arts program there." *Of course, he is.* "His name is Nicholas."

"There's a lot of people in the program, I don't really remember everyone's names." I rake my fingers through my hair, and I feel my chest sink. Before I start to tell even more lies, Jared sweeps me away.

I spend the rest of my time at the party with Jared taking a swim in the pool, and then enjoying time near the band.

We leave a little earlier than most, and when we arrive at my place, Jared follows me up to the roof of The Cake House, and we gaze at the stars.

"I hope you liked the party... and my friends," he says after a long pause of silence.

"I did, I had a lot of fun."

"Me too. So… do you visit your hometown often?"

And this is the part where I must tell him that I'm a runaway, and I just one day stopped at The Cake House, and I was offered a job and a place to stay from a complete stranger.

"I… I never go back there. I don't think I'm going to go back to my old town. My mom died when I was really young. I ran away from my abusive dad, and I ended up here. Also, Claire's not really my aunt. I met her the day she was hiring, and when I told her how I ran away, she also said I can stay here."

I'm expecting him to get up and walk away now.

"Oh, that must be really tough… having to leave everything you have ever known behind because someone was mean to you," he says instead of leaving me.

"Yeah, he used to blame me for my mom dying. He even forced me to make a video stating that it is all my fault, so he could use it against me if I ever stopped doing whatever he wanted. And I also used to wet the bed, and he made me make a video stating that I do that so he could humiliate me if necessary." Oh no, I'm oversharing. Rewind thirty seconds please, before I share the part about wetting the bed.

"Wow, that's a lot," he says and his eyes are filled with authenticity and sadness. "I envy you for having the courage to walk away from all of that."

"He would make me do everything for him, so I barely even had time to spend with friends. I don't think he wanted me to have any real friends so that I wouldn't know what being accepted by anyone else but him is like. I kept to myself a lot there, and I kind of do here too. I have Claire though." I'm not even going to mention that I think she's a psychopath too. But it dawns on me that I just shared these events of my life with Jared, and he doesn't seem to have differed in his opinion about me. I expected him to change his opinion of me, but instead he just gives the notion of simple acceptance.

He turns over, directly facing me with his hand holding his head up. He places his other hand on top of mine and holds it.

I think he can sense my discomfort in the topic, so he changes the subject.

"Do you have any future plans yet? Beyond staying here?"

"Well... I was hoping to get my G.E.D. then go to college, but I'm not even sure what I would go to college for. I was starting to want to be like Claire, and own a business like this, but now I'm not sure if that's what I'm really good at. I like art, and design seems pretty cool."

"I can see it now!" He holds his hand out, swiping it across the stars. "Elise, what's your last name again?"

"Samson," I reply.

"Elise Samson." He does another swipe over the stars. "Art Director at Cake Magazine."

"Cake Magazine?" I ask.

He shrugs. "It could happen."

We both laugh.

"I like that title."

"College is okay," he adds, "but to be honest, I am lying to my parents about going to all of my classes. I dropped two of them. I'm only going part-time now. They haven't even noticed that the bill is smaller, and I'm not really interested in becoming a lawyer like my dad." He pauses.

"I'm actually writing this story. Well, actually, it's a screenplay. I'm going to present it to HBO to become a movie. It's about this group of people that no one else interacts with that become zombies at night, so everyone has to lock their doors, and then they inject themselves with this serum and become pesky raccoons that terrorize the town during the day."

I turn myself over and face him. He sounds so serious about his story. I feel a huge smile take over my face, and I laugh a little not only because it's adorable how enthusiastic he is about writing his dreams, but also because that sounds ridiculous. He laughs a little too. "I'm almost done with it, and I read on the internet that HBO has a strict word count policy for their screenplays, it's about 40,000 words. and you have a better chance of making it a real film if you deliver it in person. I've almost reached that word count, and I'm almost ready to travel across the country and bring it to them. When I spoke to my dad about becoming a writer, he told me, I would never make it in this extremely competitive world. My mom just shrugged her shoulders, which I was assuming was in agreement. I am just really nervous about it because I want it to sell. I don't want to be so low on the scale that it ends up one of those low-quality films." He looks over at me to digest a reaction from me.

"Your excitement is really attractive." I say

"Really? Because I have never found any other girl in this world who has been so intrigued by my art! You just have to read it sometime; it would mean so much to me!"

I giggle again and glance away at the tiny specs in the sky. He takes his hand off mine and leans closer, placing it above my ear with his fingers swiping through my hair. I lean in and our lips touch. His mouth opens a little more, and he gently opens my mouth with his tongue. I can taste a mixture of stone dry angry orchard and my strawberry lip balm. There's a cool breeze that sweeps by, blowing strands of my hair so the ends tickle my cheek, and I hear the wind brushing through the trees. The crickets are singing in the background. I open my eye slightly and just in time to see a shooting star, as we continue kissing under the midnight sky.

Chapter 6

I walk into Claire's office where she's sitting down at her desk in front of her computer. First, she is elbowed down to the wood, only exposing the desktop, folders, and documents, the heel of her hands digging into her eye sockets. I ask her why I didn't get paid for my work week. She presses down on the "enter" key multiple times then leans back in her reclining leather office chair. After rubbing her eyes, massaging her temples and her cheeks, she responds.

"Oh, there must be some kind of mistake," she says, looking moderately perplexed. "I'll have to notify my new accountant of the problem, so please be patient. I've got all this new updated software I am learning how to use, and my accountant is also learning new things at the moment." She's shuffling through some papers at her desk, and she's barely made eye contact with me. I hesitate to leave with that answer alone, but with a puzzling cyclone of confusion, I do, and we both go back to work.

I'm relieved to at least hear that not getting paid was just a mistake, and I continue with my day, pushing my doubts to the back of my mind. Still having this unpleasant feeling about Claire that keeps gnawing at my brain and my gut.

Claire has hired another girl to help with orders, which I'm content with because that means I can spend some more time with Jared. Last night was magical, and I feel joyful about sharing what happened to me with him. Sharing secrets of the past with someone other than Mr. Cat-a-corn truly is as if I've released a flock of birds into the sky, and the best part is that Jared didn't judge me at all. This gives me a warm, fuzzy feeling in my chest, and it's compelling, even if a little awkward.

After I train Juliana, the new worker, Claire gives me a list of chores, such as doing a week's worth of dishes, cleaning the bathroom, and she even sent me over to her house to clean her bathroom and do her laundry. At the bottom of the list, I see the horrid words, **Damien needs a bath!** I look over at Damien rubbing up against the doorframe in the bathroom.

"Ya know what, I'm just going to pour some soapy cat shampoo and water on you and let you run around and dry off yourself." She looks up at me and gives me a mix of a growl and a loud purr. I laugh because it's as if Damien really understands what I'm saying. "I don't even know why you don't like me. I'm not trying to steal your precious mother away from you."

When the day ends, Claire lets Larry leave early, and she asks me to thoroughly clean the floors after closing.

As I kneel on the Carrara marble floor, I see Larry walk by with a 40oz Budweiser, smiling and waving. I fucking hate Claire right now, and she looked like shit today. I want my paycheck! I try to calm myself down. Taking in a deep breath, I finish my job because I'm sure if I don't, I won't get a paycheck at all.

It's that time of year again, the cake competition where Grandma chooses the family member who baked the best version of the special cakes, she keeps in her recipe book. My cousin Olivia always wins. She nailed the raspberry lemon cake last year. The year before that, it was the brown sugar peach cake, plus she made $400 selling pistachio cupcakes out of a minivan. She makes Grandma so proud. Nobody expects much from me because of my ADHD.

"Just whip up something from a Betty Crocker Box with three ingredients," they say. Well, not this time! I finger through Grandma's recipe book and land on a s'mores cake recipe. *Mmmmm*, s'mores are so tasty, so I bookmark it and save it for later. I let the headline 's'mores lovers get your taste buds ready for this marshmallow rollercoaster ride' sink in as I dose off for a couple of hours.

After my nap, I am up for some serious cake baking for the big competition. I focus, there's like thirty ingredients and five pages of instructions. This will be hard. I place my debit card in my over-the-shoulder purse and bicycle to the grocery store, securing the basket to hold the ingredients. When I gather everything, including the last bag of marshmallows on the bottom shelf of the aisle, I am confident. This is a good sign because I could focus enough to gather the items to bake this yummy cake!

The big challenge was the baking itself. I have everything set out on my kitchen counter. The recipe calls for:

1½ cups flour
tbsp. baking soda
1 tsp vanilla extract
½ tsp salt
1 cup sugar
1 cup graham cracker crumbs
1 cup water
½ cups sour cream
½ cup vegetable oil
3 eggs
1 jar hot fudge
1 jar marshmallow cream
1 cup butter cream frosting

There was more to it than I thought after going through the instructions. Soon, I have mixed up all of the ingredients, and I pour everything into two round copper cake pans, and since the oven is set to 350 degrees, I place the pans inside the oven.

I feel extra confident when I notice twenty minutes have gone by as I have been watching *Pleasantville,* the movie on television. I remove the pans from the oven, and I feel overwhelmed with the sensational marshmallow chocolate sensation with a graham cracker sugar coating scent. The cake cools soon enough, toward the end of my movie, and I frost it over with the buttercream frosting, adding marshmallows. I wish I had made it to the farmers market for some homemade buttercream frosting I had seen at a stand last week, but this will do.

It took me almost all night, but the final project is astounding. I fall asleep proud. When I awake, I feel nauseated, and I definitely did not get enough sleep last night. No amount of makeup could cover the dark circles around my eyes. I barely tried. All I could think about was my creation.

"You look like crap!" Olivia yells, grabbing the attention of the whole family as I enter the contest in the courtyard. And you look like your mom was too lazy to get out of bed the morning she was scheduled to receive an abortion. I think to myself. She's wearing a red sundress with sandal heels and her hair is beach wavy.

I place my delectable-looking s'mores cake on its place at the table. Grandma looked impressed. She was giddy when she egregiously snapped the ribbon off the post and announced that my cake had won the decorative award. Olivia got second place for decoration.

"First is the worst, second is the best," she yells in my direction.

When Grandma announces she will taste the cakes next, we all gather behind our creations. She's the lucky one who judges how delicious they are. It takes time before she arrives at my project, as she is letting her taste buds enjoy all the flavors. I have a perfect medium-sized slice waiting for her arrival.

She arrives with a smile painted on her face, and the creases of her eyes illuminate her sun-deepened wrinkles. I anticipate the moment she brings the sterling fork to her mouth. She takes a bite. I wait for the ultimate reaction! There it is. Suddenly, she couldn't breathe. She grabs at her neck with both hands as she is brought down rapidly to her knees. The whole family runs over to her, none of them pay any attention to me. She falls to the ground and chokes up blood. Everyone is doing their best to help. I watch. I forgot to mention that I added the secret ingredient... LOVE!

I wake up in a cold sweat, hyper-perplexed because I think I just had one of Claire's dreams. Like we are connected somehow. This is peculiar to me.

During the next few weeks, Jared and I drift closer together. We attend a poetry reading, a picnic in the park, we hike a mountain with a stunning waterfall and swimming hole, we have dinner at a place that serves both sushi and burgers, and sometimes we hang out in my room and watch horror films, old and new. We've both grown fond of Stephen King movies. They draw us in with words like 'spine-chilling' and 'nerve-wrenching.'

One night, we have dinner with his family. His dad is a lawyer, and his mom makes all-natural face creams, soaps, and sunscreens. She has her own catalogue. His parents are nice, but it's noticeable that they would rather see Jared with a college girl in a similar field. I can only tell because every time I felt like a conversation about my life would come up, I would down glasses of water and visit the bathroom seven times during one dinner. I made a point to spend quality time with Claire or make myself busy when Jared asks me to come around his parents again.

Jared has also begun to notice Claire's outbursts at times when he visits me. We still have our Wednesday night ritual, sometimes Julianna joins us, and sometimes I sneak away to hang out with Jared. I'm constantly sneaking out at night to visit Jared because if Claire catches me during the night, I either don't get paid for a while, or I'm stuck cleaning The Cake House and Claire's house. It has reached the point where I lie to Claire, but sometimes I'm still stuck working so hard for her approval and a place to stay.

The next workday, it seems like everyone and their mother is picking up a birthday or wedding cake. I stop to think about what mine and Jared's wedding cake will look like. I saw one in the wedding cake book with four layered cakes stacked on top of each other. They were frosted with a blend of white, blue, and green, and it looked like there were vines wrapped around the sides from the bottom to the top. There were also edible pearls around the edges. Maybe we will elope to Paris or something. Paris keeps popping up in my mind. But maybe it will be Southern France, where the villages look like something out of a *Beauty and the Beast* movie, and we can dip in the Mediterranean Sea and take a boat ride to Sardinia. Julianna catches me daydreaming, and she snaps her fingers in front of my face.

"Hello, you have a visitor," she says. "Wow, I want to hear about whatever you are thinking later because that smile on your face has mystery romance novel with a whole lotta passion written all over it."

She points to a short male with blond hair, wearing a gray hoodie. It's Jared's friend Brian.

"Uh, here ya go. Jared wanted me to give this to you." He gives a simple smile showing his dimples and rakes his hand through the side of his hair that isn't shaved. Then he hands me a note folded up into a tiny square. I undo the numerous folds, and the note says:

Run away with me. I'll come by your room later to fill you in on the details.

~ Jared

Run away with Jared? Where does he think we could be running away to? I thought I was done running away, and I just want a stable place to stay. I fold the note back up and place it in my back pocket. I look back up and see Claire open the door from the kitchen leading to the main room, and she gestures for me to come over. She wants to talk with me in her office.

"You've been working really hard for me, dear, and I really appreciate it. I'm going to offer you a $2.00 hourly raise and a bonus on this week's pay." Wow, it sounds like I'm finally appreciated for all that extra work that I'm doing. "I hope it doesn't bother you that I have been asking you to do a few extra things, I'll try to divide the work evenly between you and Julianna."

"Oh, thank you. No, it hasn't been bothering me." I'm totally lying; I've had silent thoughts about punching her sparkly white teeth out.

She lets me go early that evening, and I lie on my bed, watching another episode of *Hunter x Hunter* as I wait for Jared to come by and fill me in on the details. I don't know if I can run away with him when I have a stable place to stay and a job. I also don't want him to leave though.

I think I may even be falling in love with him. If I even know what love really is! But what if we run away, and it doesn't work out? Claire would never take me back in. Maybe someone else would take this studio shortly after I leave. My dreams of having a mother figure back in my life will also be over. I mean, sure Claire seems jealous if I'm spending time with someone who makes me happy, but she has a good side too.

There's a knock at my door. I open it up, and Jared barges in excitedly.

"I've finished my screenplay! I can bring it to HBO! You can run away with me to Los Angeles, get your G.E.D., and become an actor in my movie! This would be perfect for you!"

I blink hard several times. He's pacing around happily, like he has a sugar high, and I'm waiting for him to realize the absurdity of his words on his own. He doesn't. He walks circles around my room, using a collection of words to make his point sound feasible.

"Maybe I will make it into a series! Oh, boy this is going to be so good!"

"You really think this could work?" I ask almost in a whisper.

"Sure, it will, and I don't want to be a lawyer. Claire treats you like an unworthy maid sometimes. Plus, you are a runaway anyway. So, let's do it! Run away with me, Elise." He drops down to one knee and holds his hand out.

I'm a runaway anyway? As if I like running and the anxiety of not knowing what's going to happen? I can't believe he just said that to me. I'm a bit infuriated. Plus, Claire is sorry about all the work she has made me do lately and offered me a raise and a bonus on top of this room.

"Look, just think about it." He gets back up on his feet, reaches into his back pocket and hands me an envelope, it's heavy with his printed story that makes no sense. "This is my screenplay I was telling you about." He's panting from pacing the room. "When you have the chance, read it. I'm going to start making plans to leave, I'll come back when I have decided on a date." Jared gives me a quick kiss on the cheek and hurries out of the door, and I close it behind him. This is a lot to take in. I'll read Jared's story later, I suppose. In the meantime, I decide to lie back down and continue watching the seasons of *Hunter x Hunter* until I fall asleep.

Chapter 7

When I awake, I sit upright in my bed, and look at the large manila envelope on my nightstand for a few minutes. *Should I read his story and then decide if it's worth it to run away? Do I kind of want to run away with Jared even if his story doesn't turn into an HBO movie?* A change of scenery sounds kind of nice. Palm trees and salty sea air, warm sand between my toes and a Ferris wheel upon the Santa Monica Pier. Disney Land!

I could end up with a job that pays less and doesn't offer a home and food like Claire. Plus, Jared would be so depressed if HBO doesn't like his screenplay. The kind of depression that Space Mountain may not be able to cure. Jared is so sweet to me, and I think I have real feelings for him, but do I really want to run away again? Pleasurable memories of what he said about getting my G.E.D. scurry their way into my hippocampus. He does know how badly I want my G.E.D.

It's a typical Saturday, leftover croissants from the bakery, and CBS Saturday morning plays in the background as I run the Swiffer across the hardwood floors of my room. I haven't heard from Jared though, which is displeasing. I call his home line, but his mom tells me she hasn't seen him since late last night. There's a sudden ring of my phone line, and it's Julianna at the other end. I remember that I told her she can contact me on our days off. I got paid, plus my $200 bonus this week.

Our final decision plans are to make it out to the mall and

take a break for lunch at Red Robin in the food court. Julianna is eighteen, but she still lives with her foster parents. She says they are always drunk or passed out, so she pretty much takes care of herself. It's like we have more in common than I thought.

"Yeah, so like, it really doesn't make much sense that the state of Massachusetts placed me in a foster care that is literally almost like my biological parents' home except they were poor, and this family is rich. It's like taking a child from poor alcoholic drug dealers and giving it to rich alcoholics who buy drugs just because they have jobs. But whatever, I'm alive, right? I have my own room, and I can eat brand name cereal and wash my hair with shampoo and conditioner in separate bottles." She takes a sip of her diet Pepsi.

I never would have guessed she was in foster care. She's clean, her nails are always trimmed and painted, her hair is perfectly highlighted with three different shades of blonde that shine when the light illuminates it. Her teeth are perfectly straight as if she once had braces, and if someone were to rob her on the street, they would make a killing off her jewelry alone. I always thought kids in foster care aren't taken care of.

"So, who's that cute guy that's always coming in to see you?" she asks right before taking a bite of her monster burger. "Does he have any brothers? Friends? Cousins?" We both laugh.

"He's someone I just started hanging around with a few months ago… we are… kinda dating. We hang out a lot together."

"Yeah, Claire says you used to spend more Wednesday nights with her until he came around. I like Claire, she's like the coolest boss."

Wait, Claire talks about Jared and me with Julianna?

"Ya, Claire's awesome." Well, she is when Jared isn't

around and when I don't have to do my job, Larry's job, and her housework. See, Julianna likes both Claire and Jared, I wish they would start liking each other.

We finish our delightful burgers. "Lunch is on me." Julianna insists as she holds her hand out to stop me from pulling out some cash from my purse.

"You don't have to do that, Julianna."

"Another perk to living with rich parents who barely care what goes on in your life." She yanks out a platinum Chase visa card from her Gucci wallet. I suppose I allow her to treat me. She grins devilishly.

After our meals are paid for, and I leave some cash for a tip, we continue to window shop for a bit.

We walk into Abercrombie, and I watch Julianna eyeball a scarf that she likes and grabs it off the shelf. It's a silverish color polyester scarf with a glittery accent.

"$22.99 for a scarf? As if!" She rolls the scarf up into a ball between both hands and stuffs it into her Wet Seal shopping bag with items she purchased before eating lunch. I give her a wide-eyed look and raise my brows, as if to gesture an "are you serious" expression without vocalizing it. So now I know how Julianna covers herself with updated clothing and accessories.

"That's nothing," she whispers, reaching out her hand and wrapping her fingers around my wrist, pulling me closer so she can speak softly in my ear and no one else can hear. With her other hand, she points over at the wall. "You see some of these tank tops? They don't even have anyone working the dressing rooms most of the time; we can layer some underneath what we are wearing." I look in the direction she points me in. I've never stolen anything from a store before, and there are some appealing tops hung up on a display wall that I wouldn't mind snatching for free.

Chapter 8

It's been almost a week since I have seen or heard from Jared, and I'm wondering what is going on as well as feeling anxious to hear about his plans to run away to LA. I'm starting to like that I have another friend at The Cake House, and things with Claire seem to be back to normal. I miss Jared though, and nothing really tops the time that we spend together. I don't even know what I am going to say the next time he shows up with his talk about zombies and raccoons.

I think back to how Jared's eyes light up when he talks about his story, and how he really wants HBO to see it and share it with the world. I also think about the time we have spent together, not just the times we have spent going out and having fun, but the times we have spent in my room, alone together. We haven't had sex yet, we've only made out and have gotten to second base, but most of all I love the way he holds me close at night, and how he lies next to me and listens while he runs his fingers through my hair and twirls them through the strands. The thought sends a shiver of euphoria down my spine. It's official. I need Jared!

Oh my God, this whole time I've been worried about seeing him because he wants me to run away again, but now I'm even more anxious because we haven't connected all week. He could have moved on without me. Maybe he decided to leave already. I've been so busy making sure Claire is happy, I haven't even thought about what Jared may be up to and wonder if he is still really going to come back for me.

Trying to fall asleep is a struggle when night falls. I try watching television and then I try reading an article I printed out at the library about Sigmund Freud and his theory on dreams. I have come to the conclusion that I do not understand Freudian language. It sounds like he just goes around in circles, using a collection of made-up words to make his point sound feasible. All I can really gather is that everyone dreams whether we remember it or not. So, on the nights where I dream something pleasant, I wake up with nothing on my conscious mind, yet I wake up from a bad dream with the ability to shovel out every last detail? This is complete horse shit!

I become lured in by the title *Lucid Dreams*. This, Freud points out, is when we are in the midst of the dream, yet we are aware that we are dreaming. During this process, we have control over changing the dream. Interesting! I make a mental note of that.

I try to stretch, spray some lavender, and I even try counting sheep. As I watch the white bundles of cotton jump one-by-one above my head and over to the other side, I toss and I turn, and I end up staring at my alarm clock watching every minute go by and then every hour. When I wake up in the morning, I'm like a zombie who is too tired to chase after some brains.

That day Brian comes into The Cake House, and I catch him chatting with Julianna while he orders a slice of cheesecake and some chocolate mousse, so I walk over to say hi.

"Hey, Brian!" Brian gives a light wave and then glances down at the floor. I wonder what that means. When Julianna hands him his treats, he hurries outside and hops into his silver Mazda parked on the side street in front of the building. That was strange. Julianna glances over at me with an I'm so sorry I'm about to give you some unpleasant information look as she slightly pouts her lips.

"What is it?" I ask, placing my hands on my hips, questioning if I even want to know.

"Your dad is in town, and I just found out he's paying Jared to take you out and date you. Then…" At first, I haven't even processed what just came out of Julianna's mouth. I feel numb and surprisingly calm as I await the next thing, she's about to tell me. Why would Julianna and Brian be talking about my dad? And why the fuck would Jared be involved with my dad? *My dad sent a gorgeous guy to come spend time with me and show me that he cares about me?* I don't get it.

"Then Jared is supposed to kidnap you and take you back to him, and Jared will have enough money to move to Los Angeles and start a new life." She, too, looks down at the floor, saddened by the news she had to break to me.

A cyclone of fury is taking over my insides, and I can feel my heart beating against my chest. I'm angry and anxious with the realization that now I do have to run away again without Jared. And it's all because of fucking Jared! My dad probably knows where I work now. My mouth goes dry and I'm starting to sweat. I run to the bathroom to splash cold water on my face and get it together so I can finish my workday. *Where am I going to go next?*

I walk out of the bathroom and walk back to where Julianna is standing at the register.

"Look, Julianna, I'm not feeling that well. I'm going to stay in the back, cleaning and doing the dishes. Just let me know if you really need my help out here."

"Okay. Sorry I had to break the news to you." She frowns.

"Are you sure you don't want me to tell Claire you feel sick so you can go back up to bed? You are looking a little pale."

I turn around and head to the back room.

"What the fuck. Why did I let Jared into my life to take advantage of me?" I whisper to myself as I start scrubbing the dishes.

"Ouch." I reach into the hot soapy water and pull out a serrated knife. This is why we aren't supposed to soak them in the sink full of water. My finger is oozing with blood that rapidly drips down the rest of my hand.

I reach for a hand towel and apply pressure. Then I turn around to find Claire standing, staring at me with her arms crossed.

"You do know that is why sharp objects are not supposed to be submerged in soapy water."

"Yes, I have just been having a rough day so far." I sigh heavily.

"Follow me, I will clean you up." I follow Claire to the room where she keeps the first aid supplies. She wraps my finger in a bandage, and then I go back and join Julianna in the bakery.

When my workday ends, I race up to my room without saying anything to anyone before I go. I start packing my backpack again, and again I'm pained with the thoughts of another man hurting me. This one was so different though. And I'm so upset with myself because I shared so much of myself with Jared. I lie down on my bed with my face in my pillow, squeezing Mr. Cat-a-corn because I just can't bring myself to do anything right now.

Suddenly, there's a loud knock on my door. I freeze now because I'm too scared to even ask who it is. Whoever it is they keep banging, and they don't stop.

"Elise! It's Jared! Please open up!" Oh my God, I can't believe he would show up here right now! I remain quiet. A pin dropping to the floor right now would sound like a window breaking. "Listen, Elise, if you're in there, you must understand that you are in danger right now. We both are! Please listen to me," he shouts in a panic.

"Why should I listen to you? I told you everything about my dad, and then I find out that you have been working for him! You have been using me! For him!"

"Look, your dad was offering me money to get you to like me, and then bring you back to him, but I thought you were just being a spoiled brat not listening to your dad because he has you on a curfew or makes you clean your room. Now I know he's the problem."

"That's great, I wonder how you found out, genius! You sure as hell didn't trust me!"

"I know, I was wrong, please listen to me. He wanted me to tie you up and restrain you and then bring you to him, and I said that was too much. Physically restraining someone and forcing them to go see a person they don't want to see is taking it too far. So, I declined. And I started to remember everything you told me, and the pain in your eyes.

"I started to feel your pain, Elise. He took me to his friend's house, and we were in his garage. When I said I wouldn't do it to you, and that I loved you, his friend offered to take on the mission. I was filled with rage that someone was going to do that to you, so I grabbed the gun out of your dad's pocket, and I shot him. I ran away, and your dad hasn't been able to find me, but he was yelling threats that he was going to kill me. I kept running. Please let me in. Look, I did get $10,000 from him, we can still run away to LA. I meant what I said about you coming with me, I just thought I was doing a good deed while making some extra cash reuniting a father and a daughter who may just have mixed feelings! I would never tie you up and force you to go somewhere with someone who hurt you so much." He's bawling his eyes out on the other side of the door.

"Okay, I'll let you in." I look around first and reach for a hammer that I use to nail down my LED lights I left on a shelf next to the door. "I have a weapon; in case, this is a trick."

"Please, Elise, it's not a trick. We are in real danger." I take a deep breath in and slowly release the air back out. I gently turn the lock in the door, turn the doorknob with my eyes sealed shut, then quickly grip the hammer with both hands and bounce back away as he steps in. He very slowly steps in, revealing that he has a gun, but carefully places it on the floor. He shuts the door behind him.

"You have a gun?"

"Yes, I told you, I shot the man that was going to tie you up and take you to your dad. I took it from your dad."

"Okay," I say, shaking with my hammer still tightly gripped in both hands. He steps toward me. "Don't come any closer!" I screech. He backs away with his hands out where I can see them.

"Elise, we must leave, we can start heading West tonight and stop at a hotel if we need to. I've already researched the location of the HBO studios and we have enough money to rent a place in the area."

"OH MY GOD, JARED! You really think you are going to make it big in Hollywood with the zombie raccoons you have created?" I'm still so angry that now I don't have much of a choice but to leave with the man who betrayed me for my dad. Tears fill up the ducts in his eyes, and he looks broken. It's as if I'm a raven who just pierced my beak right through his heart. *But what about what he did to my heart?*

I begin to calm down a little, understanding what Jared is going through. It is hard to stay mad at Jared. My dad put him up to this. And he killed a guy who was going to harm me.

"I'll go with you," I whisper.

Chapter 9

The air is crisp as we drive away from The Cake House and start heading West. I unwrap the slice of coffee cake held in a napkin and pinch pieces of it into my mouth. My comfort food, and my reward to myself for taking the next step. It's still warm, and I am inhaling the sweet cinnamon scent as I brush the strands of hair poking at my face and the light breeze flows in from the cracked window. I watch hastily through Jared's rearview mirror as the sign of The Cake House gets smaller and disappears as we change streets. We only make it a few blocks before I hear a loud ticking sound from the engine of the Honda Civic.

"Should we maybe pull over and check what that sound is?" I ask. I crunch up my face and pinch my nose as the smell of gas hits the interior.

"Oh, is that coming from my car?" Jared asks.

"Um, well this is a back road, and I don't see any other cars around." I shrug, and then I roll the window down further on my side and peek my head outside just in case I'm wrong.

Jared pulls over into the driveway of what looks like it leads to a boat ramp, and we stop to take a break. Jared pops the trunk and pulls out a flashlight and some oil he has stored there.

"It might just be low on oil." He shrugs as he comes around to the driver side window, opens the door, and proceeds to pop the hood. "I'll get an oil change in the morning I suppose after we find a place to stay."

I nod and gaze out my window, listening to the cicadas, the

crickets, and faint sound of tiny waves brushing onto the rocks and the sand. Jared closes the hood after he adds the oil and gets back into the car. We both pause a little, listening to what nature has to offer. It's clear that we're both tired and stressed. I feel a sharp pain in the upper right side of my head. We are silent, both lost in our thoughts, and it takes a few minutes before I let out a loud burp.

We both laugh. "Oops. I guess it broke the silence though."

Amid our laughter, someone creeps up to the car. Slowly I turn my head to look out the back window, but I see nothing. Just as I turn my head back around, someone snaps open my door, aggressively shoving a cloth bag over my head like I'm some potato. Before I have time to see their face, he wraps his arms tightly around me, pulling me out of the car. I recognize this forceful arm hold. He continues to pull me out of the car as I'm screaming at the top of my lungs. Jared is pulling my legs, and it is as if he is playing a painful game of tug of war with his favorite toy he can't let go of and a highly aggressive pit-bull.

The man, I'm assuming is Dad at this point, manages to drag me out of the car, and he falls to the ground, still holding me tight. He picks us both back up, and as I'm struggling to make him release me, he holds on tighter like I'm involuntarily squeezed into a big bear hug. Oh God, I hate when adults use the term "bear hug" as if it's suddenly going to become appealing and persuade children to enjoy becoming a slave to some asshole by allowing them to wrap their repulsive arms around them.

Then, suddenly, I hear a gunshot and we both collapse. He falls flat on the ground, and I fall down on top of him.

I swiftly pull the bag off my head and back away from him. My dad is holding his wound on his left side with both hands. The blood just keeps pouring out and he's shaking. I don't know what to say or do. It's dark, and the only light upon us are the moon, the specs of stars in the autumn sky, and the interior light from the driver and passenger doors of the open car. Jared walks over, and I can hear the cracking of twigs and pebbles under his boots. He stands over my dad, aiming the gun directly at him.

My heart sinks as I wait for what Jared is going to do. He looks vicious and angry, as if the full moon has summoned a werewolf inside of him. Dad is shaking, and it looks like he's searching for the words to say to make Jared forgive him. My mouth has gone dry.

Even if I want to say something, I'm restricted. Even if I want to feel something in this moment, I am also restricted. All I can do is watch. Even if I want to stop what I know Jared is on the verge of doing, I can't. It's like I'm in the audience of a theater, and the only thing I can do is watch.

Jared puts his finger on the trigger, panting heavily. He pulls the trigger, and the shot fires, piercing through my dad's forehead, and blood splatters all over the place I'm still trembling as I shoot myself up from the ground. When I stand, I'm frozen in place as I stare into Jared's rage-filled eyes that suddenly look just as shocked as I am. He doesn't say anything. He puts the gun down, hooks his arms through my dad's, holding him from underneath his armpits and drags him toward the lake. He's covered in blood, and his head hangs down, chin touching his chest. I decide to help Jared by picking up my dad's legs. Ewe, it feels so gross holding a lifeless body. When we reach the water, we push him in, and the dark water swallows him whole.

We both stop and look at each other, then we rush back to Jared's car, and he struggles to steady his hand and put the key in the ignition. When he turns the key, it starts smoothly. We both look at each other, waiting for the ticking sound, but it's inaudible.

"See, it just needed a little oil." He looks at me and gives a nervous laugh.

I'm silent as we back our way out of the driveway and onto the road.

"Jared, I want you to take me back to The Cake House." He pulls a look, and his eyebrows furrow before he becomes wide-eyed in agreement.

"Okay, good idea. We can stay there tonight and leave in the morning."

"No, I want to stay there alone tonight. If you want to leave without me, that's fine, but I will give you a call if I decide that I'm ready to go with you."

"Okay," he says sadly. "I'm sorry that there's blood all over your nice tank top, it looks new."

"It's fine, I stole it when I went shopping with Julianna, the girl I work with at The Cake House."

"You've been shoplifting? With someone Claire's hired at The Cake House? See, Claire invites you around bad influences and treats you poorly when someone good comes around. Why do you want to go back there?"

I purse my lips and bite my cheek.

"Jared, you were working for my abusive dad, who hired you to get information from me about HIM and then wanted you to get me to go back there with him until YOU decided you didn't trust him around me, so you killed his friend, pissed him off and left him with all of my information. You're really not in a position to judge Claire right now or anyone she associates with."

He's speechless after I'm done speaking, and we both stay silent the rest of the way. When we arrive at The Cake House, I insist on walking myself to my room.

"I do appreciate you saving me from that guy and my dad." I look into Jared's depressing puppy dog eyes. "I will call you. If you decide to go to L.A. without me, you can keep in touch with me. Maybe I will even meet you out there. Please understand that I just need a little bit of time."

"I understand," he says, and I lean in to give him a soft kiss.

Stepping out of the car, I bite my bottom lip, wondering if I have just made a mistake. Nervous that I may never see Jared again. No, this decision is definitely for the best. I wave to him from the sidewalk, as a cool breeze sweeps through my hair, and he drives off into the darkness. I turn and rush up the stairs to the shower that awaits me, then I try to push aside any thoughts of doubt before I drift into a deep sleep.

I wake up in the middle of the night in the top floor of the barn Aunt Monica and Maryanne told Olivia and I to sleep together in. This was our annual summer trip to Vermont. It was not always paradise. Sure, Maryanne made delicious blueberry pancakes, bacon, and eggs. We also get to make s'mores by the campfire, but I was always stuck rooming with Olivia, and we just happened to get picked to sleep in the barn where there was no bathroom around except for an outhouse outside that you had to walk down the stairs into the pitch black forest and creep around the side of the barn only to reach out your arms, using touch as a form of sight to get to.

There were always wolves howling, snakes slithering, and of course bears could be roaming around at night, just waiting for a skinny little red head to step outside so they can devour an evening snack. I had to go to the bathroom, and it was not to go pee. Aunt Monica told me and Olivia to wake each other up if we needed to use the outhouse. Well, here goes.

"Olivia," I whisper. She's snoring. "Olivia, please I need to go to the bathroom," I whisper again. Then I shove the covers to one side and shift my body out of bed. We were in two twin-sized beds with an end table separating them. There was a small lamp on the table, so I switched it on. I tip-toe toward Olivia and give her a little push.

"Olivia, I really need to use the bathroom," I whine this time because I really have to go now.

"I am tired, stop touching me, I am trying to sleep." She rolls over to the other side.

"But we were supposed to go together if one of us needs to go. I am not going out there by myself. Oliva, c'mon." She says nothing. Olivia would not budge. I take a deep breath. *Am I really going to have to wander out there alone?* I turn my head to see a large white bucket in the corner of the room. I bite the side of my bottom lip. It seems I really have no other choice. There could be a masked murderer out there standing in the dark by the fireplace! All that surrounds us is forest!

I just do it. I do number two in the bucket, and that's all there is to it. There was toilet paper there because we could go pee in the bucket, but number two was supposed to be done in the outhouse. After I did it, I turned the switch of the lamp off, and I crawled back into bed. Sorry, Olivia, but I really had to go.

When the sun rises the next morning, Olivia and I both head off to breakfast, but there is one thing I forget. It probably would have been best to hide the fact that I did number two in the bucket because after breakfast, Monica sees that it had been done. After breakfast is no picnic because Maryanne and Monica scream at me in front of all of the other cousins. What a vacation! I spend the rest of the afternoon alone in my room feeling sorry for myself. It was Olivia's fault. She wouldn't come to the outhouse with me. *Why am I so wrong for being scared of the dark outside when no one else was around?*

It doesn't seem like very long before the alarm starts buzzing. There you have it; I had another one of Claire's dreams last night. This is getting out of control. I feel sorry for Claire. Maybe these things really happened to her. Anyhow, it probably isn't best for me to stay here with her, catching her dreams. This is something she must sort out on her own.

I go to work like nothing happened. I either don't feel anything or I'm avoiding any feelings toward both Jared betraying me and my dad being gone for good. I stay a little later to help Claire organize her recipe books so we can close up together. I think I just needed that one night to myself because as soon as I head up to my room, I'm going to call Jared. To be honest, I hope he hasn't left yet because I think I'm ready to start a new life with him. He really did save me, even if he put me in danger in the first place.

Claire peeks her head in the office while I finish putting the last recipe binder together. She tilts her head and smiles.

"I'm just going to put the closed sign up and lock up before I leave. Do you need anything?"

"No, I'm good. I'm almost done here."

She gives me a sharp look like she's impressed with me and walks back into the bakery. Minutes pass, and as I'm placing the binder into Claire's filing cabinet, I hear a loud bang followed by ominous silence. *What just happened? Did Claire fall or something? Is she in danger?* I hurry out to help her, and I see Claire standing with a large crystal vase filled with yellow daisies from one of the cafe tables above her head, and Jared is lying face down on the floor! *What... the... fuck? If I move, is Claire going to kill me too?* It's like one of those horror movies where the crazy person is revealed and just doesn't care any more and goes around killing everyone in sight! For a split second I feel courageous, and I race over to him anyway, turning him over on his back.

He has a huge gash on his head, and blood is dripping rapidly down his face! I check his neck for a pulse. I don't find one. Jared's dead! Claire killed him. He's gone, and his dreams of selling his story to HBO died with him. Claire doesn't say anything at all. She lowers the vase, places it back on the table, and wipes her hands on her apron. I'm on my knees in tears.

"Why did you do this? He was so young. He had dreams. How could you?" Rivers of tears flow down my cheeks, giving me blurred vision. "He didn't do anything to you!" Claire doesn't answer me. "You have nothing to say? You're just going to stand there? What, are you going to make me clean up this mess too, Claire?" All I can see is her blurry face drowned in my tears. "I hate you! You ruined my plans! You ruined everything!" At this point, I'm expecting her to come after me and kill me too, but she does nothing.

I was ready to run away with him. I realize right then as I look at him lying lifeless on the marble floor with blood nearly covering his entire beautiful face that I now know what I'm going to do. I'm going to take Jared's story to HBO and present it as my own. That's what Jared would have wanted! He came back here for me. *And Claire killed him... for me?*

Chapter 10

My alarm goes off at 9.48 a.m. the next day, and as I lift my head up and hustle to raise my eyelids, I'm pained by a splitting headache. I place the palm of my hand on my forehead, my eyes only slightly cracked open. My arm is slathered in dry, cracking mud, there are strands of grass stuck to my skin.

I can barely see my room through the blur as my eyelids are awakening slowly. My mind shifts to last night. Jared's dead body on the floor and the blood flowing like rivers from the gash on the top of his head and trickling down his face. I slowly raise my comforter up revealing the rest of my body and the fact that both of my hands and arms are dirty. I'm still wearing my khakis from work the night before, and they are bloodstained with a graveyard fade at the bottom, matching my socks. Well, at least I remembered to take my shoes off last night before crawling into my off-white satin sheets.

Claire hasn't come upstairs to wake me this morning, and I'm just dreading going back down into the bakery and seeing her after what she did to Jared. How could she take his life? And why do I look like I helped bury the remains with no memory of the rest of the night? I look over at Jared's story, still in the envelope. I never took the time to read it, and I want to share it with HBO because Jared was so exhilarated with the thought of bringing it there and thrilled to have me come there with him. I just must get it there. Tomorrow... I can pack up and hop on the first bus at the bus station heading West.

I finally find the strength to pull myself out of bed. My head is still spinning and throbbing. I put one hand on my nightstand for balance and my middle and pointer fingers back on my forehead. I take a deep breath, and I try to clear my mind of thoughts that only amplify the throbbing pain in my head. First, I need to find a way to feel better, then I can collect my thoughts about the night before and figure out what happened and what I'm going to do next.

There is a strong breeze coming from my window, blowing through my hair, and filling my lungs with fresh air. It's satisfying. The smell of pumpkin spice and cinnamon apple evaporates from the bakery into my room. I boost my head up so that I can make my way into the kitchen. My body is gently swaying as I creep over to the sink to get myself a cup of water. I turn the knob on the faucet and let the water run cold. Grabbing a cup sitting on the counter, I fill it halfway. I take a couple of sips and place it back down, leaving fingerprints of filth on the glass.

It's a simpler walk to the bathroom where I turn the shower on. It's too much for me to stand, so I sit in the bathtub with the cool water spraying from the shower head sprinkling over me, watching the dirty water run down the drain. I grab my loofa and scrub with soap until my skin is back to the pale white pigment it has always been. My blurred vision clears a bit, and I turn the water off, lift myself up, and wrap a towel around my weak and fragile body.

When I conjure up the strength, I put on a pair of comfortable clothes, brush my teeth, and throw my hair in a bun that sits right on top of my head. I stare at myself in the bathroom mirror for a few minutes, gazing at my tired eyes with dark circles around them.

"What I saw last night had to have been a dream," I say to myself. "Please, God, tell me this was only a dream."

Ya, that must be it. I had a dream about Jared getting hit over the head and watching him lying on the floor covered in blood. I must have slept-walked outside into a mud pile. That makes perfect sense.

Oh my God, what I remember and what I woke up to don't match up at all. And I'm dreading any future encounters with Claire. I close my eyes again and tell myself there is nothing to worry about and that everything will be okay. Then I dab some concealer on to cover the dark spots, add a layer of mascara to my lashes, and convince myself to walk downstairs to The Cake House.

When I get downstairs, Julianna is standing at the cash register filing her nails. She pauses and glances over at me as I emerge from the door and into the bakery. She raises her thinly plucked eyebrows and grins.

"Hi, sleepy head."

"Where's Claire?" I ask as I storm into the room, come to a halt right before her, placing one hand on my hips, and the other on the glass cake shelf tapping each fingernail on the glass simultaneously. There's no one else in the room.

"She's in her office, whyyy?" She scans me up and down, and she's wearing a confused look as if I'm an angry spouse searching for our teenage daughter with evidence that she did something wrong, and Julianna's supposed to know what she did and how to fix it. I give her a stern and paranoid stare.

"I think we might be in danger," I whisper, darting my eyes to the door that leads to Claire's office and then back to Julianna. She drops her nail file on the counter, narrows her brows, creasing her forehead. She presses her lips together and gives me a dead look.

"Elise, what are you talking about?"

I place my two hands on both of her shoulders. "You are going to have to trust me on this one. Something bad happened, Julianna, something really bad happened." I lift my hands off her shoulders and start pacing behind the cake shelf, biting my nails.

"What is it? What happened? You must tell me now. You're freaking me out." Julianna starts to panic.

Suddenly, the entrance door swings open, and a man and a woman enter. The woman has dirty blonde wavy hair, that flows about an inch past her shoulders, and is casually dressed in black pants and a floral print tunic. A gold-colored scarf is draped around her neck, and she's wearing natural makeup. The man she is with is tall with broad shoulders, dark hair, and olive skin. He's wearing a black dress shirt tucked into a pair of tan chinos. They both approach the register, with looks of seriousness and determination. The man removes his blue tinted ray bans and places them atop his head.

"We're looking for a girl named Elise Samson," he says in a deep, authoritative voice. Julianna and I are silent and Julianna's immediate resistance to turn directly toward me and remove her eyes from the officers tells me she is waiting for my response so she can follow.

"We don't know an Elise Sampson. At least I don't think we do. *Hmm*, give me a sec. Julianna… do we know anyone by the name of Elise Samson?" I say, shrugging my shoulders, the ends of my lips pointing downwards and shaking my head, delegating the question over to my fellow colleague.

"Nope, that name doesn't ring a bell at all," Julianna says nervously.

"Then you might want to explain why you look exactly like

Elise." The girl detective pulls out my most recent school portrait, waving it right in front of my face. Damn it, I should have known that a couple of government agents would have easy access to a picture of their target person. It's a great picture of me actually, my hair parted perfectly to the left, my wispy bangs hung just above my eyelid, and a glowing, dimpled smile that reaches my eyes. I sure could look happy in front of a camera. But that's beside the point... why are they looking for me? Jared killed my dad, and Claire killed Jared. I didn't kill anyone.

My lips open, my arms tighten against the sides of my body and both hands form fists with my nails digging into my palms. I start to feel hot and panicky, and I feel the perspiration seep from my hair line. The walls are closing in, and it is like I'm suffocating. I don't say anything at all. I don't even know what to say because a dead guy killed my dad. A dead guy that I loved, and now I'm being blamed for it.

The detective gives a quick nod at her partner, and he nods back. She stampers around the cake shelf and walks toward me with aggression and perseverance. The loud tapping of her ankle-high low-heeled boots are exasperating as she approaches me. She pulls a set of handcuffs out of her belt loop, grabs my wrist and clasps it with one metal cuff then reaches for my other wrist and does the same. With both hands behind my back, she squeezes both arms just above the steel rings chained together to tightly secure my compliance.

"You are under arrest as a suspect in the murder of your father, Jason Samson. You have the right to remain silent, anything you say can and will be used against you in the court of law." I lock eyes with Julianna, and her expression tells me she wishes there was something she can do, but she says nothing. Our eyes remain locked as I'm being dragged away from her, trying to suction the souls of my vans to the floor to resist cooperatively walking backward, like a toddler who refuses to leave the toy aisle, resulting in a forceful departure induced by the parent. The back door slams open. Claire must have heard the commotion because she steps out from the opening and places her palms to her cheek. Her mouth drops open.

"What... what is going on here?" she yelps, hurrying over to us before the officer pulls me outside. "There has to be some kind of mistake, what is going on here?"

Ya don't worry Claire, your secret about killing Jared is safe with me.

Mr. Don't Question Me man cop jumps in front of her, flashing his badge again right in her face, waving his other arm, signaling girl cop to continue hauling me outside.

"We are removing this girl because she is a suspect in a murder investigation. That is all we can say to you right now. She is being taken to Ludlow. Have a nice day, ma'am."

I give up resisting, and we step out into the bright, sunlit sidewalk on the street where The Cake House is set. The air is cool, and my eyes are squinting due to the brightness of the warm sun, and I feel naked with nothing disguising me as I'm being taken away in handcuffs. Every driver comes to a halt to look in my direction.

The woman guides me to an unmarked police vehicle parked on the side of the street and opens the rear-passenger side door, giving a light hand bump to my elbow, gesturing me to hop inside. I do so, and she buckles me in. The interior smells like Armor All and destruction. She closes the door and gets in the car. Boy cop hops in the passenger side shortly after. There are bars behind their car seats that separate us. I sigh and press the side of my forehead up against a bar on the window, take one look at The Cake House sign and the dessert in the window, and we drive away.

Farms with tractors outside fertilizing the land, some wide-open fields with emerald hills are in the background, a strip mall, and a cemetery all blur by, my forehead still pressed against the steel bars in this gruesome, ominous car ride of doom. *This should be Claire's ride to hell.* I think to myself, wishing this was all just another dream.

Chapter 11

We pull into the parking lot of a tall brick building with small windows labeled Ludlow Detention Center. When the car is parked, both cops remove their seatbelts. I lift my head up from the window bars in a panic. There's a soreness on my forehead from leaning up against the metal.

"Wait, I can't be here. I'm a juvenile. I'm only seventeen. I don't turn eighteen for another two months."

"Two months?" The man turns his neck to the side, and his eyes shift toward me. "It's November 4, our records show that you turned eighteen yesterday. You're being charged as an adult."

"No, I'm not an adult. I'm just a kid."

"You are young and possibly naïve. But in the eyes of the law, you are an adult. Two months wasn't really going to matter anyway."

His words go right through me, cutting like a scalpel, and I'm numb on anesthetic so I don't even know how to feel. It doesn't make any sense to me and doesn't feel real. No one else was around the night my dad tried to take me out of Jared's car and he got shot. We threw the gun far enough into the water, and even if it was found, my fingerprints were never on it. All I can do is let out a sigh and hope that sooner rather than later, I will be exposed to the answers to all the questions I have ruminating around in my head.

The man turns away again, and both officers open their doors and step out of the vehicle. The woman opens my door and escorts me out of the car, and with her hand firmly holding one arm, she walks me toward the building. When we reach the door, there is one male police officer outside with a strong build, wearing a navy-blue uniform with a gold-colored badge and the letters LCPD engraved on it. He nods at us. At first, he opens his mouth and looks like he's about to say something, but he doesn't. His eyes just follow mine as we walk inside. When we enter, I'm briefly freed from the cuffs. I massage my wrists before moving any further, giving them a brief moment of freedom, and then I meet two guards in uniform who have me walk through a metal detector as they make small talk with the detectives.

The room is large with different shades of gray. Whoever decorated this place didn't have much of an imagination. It is lit up but still feels dark. There's a visitor area with stainless steel round tables connected to stainless steel stools to my left. A cafeteria seems to be hidden behind a door to my right where I see the tops of heads and hairnets moving around through a thin, rectangular glass window.

Many other closed doors are in sight from where I stand, and after passing through security, I'm taken into another gray room for fingerprints and a photoshoot. Next, the detectives slap my cuffs back on and bring me into a small, gently lit room with a conference table in the middle. Dust floats around, lingering in the dim light. The air is stale and cold, and I'm overwhelmed with feelings of sadness as my heart sinks down into depression.

My cuffs are once again removed, and I stretch my arms a bit. I look over at the two, and the woman uses her eyes and chin to direct me to the one chair on the opposite side of the table as the man walks out. She pulls her chair out to take a seat. I pull my chair out, and the legs make a screeching sound on the floor like nails on a chalkboard, sending goosebumps up my arm and a quiver throughout my body. I plop onto the cold piece of metal, leaning back to get comfortable, but the chair feels rough against my shoulder blades and spine. I lean forward again, lace both hands together in front of me on the table and look cautiously into the woman's eyes, feeling the weight of her heavy stare.

"I'm detective Emma Michaud, and I will be interviewing you concerning the relationship you had with your father. Let's just see here." She flips her fingers through some papers that look disorganized in front of her. She shuffles back and forth between sections of paperwork. Her glasses are slipping down her nose. "Okay, let's start here. His body was found by an eight-year-old who was walking her poodle out to the dock by her family's cabin." She gives me a fierce stare after reading that one sentence, probably looking for some sort of immediate reaction in my eyes. I don't budge. "Oh, don't worry." She raises her palm up. "It says here that the eight-year-old wasn't harmed, it turns out she has some fascination with horror and violence."

She slaps her hand back down on the table, releasing the paperwork and repositioning her body from legs-crossed and relaxed to leaning in toward me, pressing her lips together as she continues. "We've talked to neighbors, teachers, and administration at Portsmouth High School, located in... New Hampshire. Is that right?" I nod my head indicating that the answer is yes. "People who work with your father at the medical supply factory have been concerned. It seems that your father has been looking for you after a violent outburst you had ending with a bookcase you shoved on top of him, landing on his face. He was really banged up and heartbroken is what everyone says. And it seems you've made yourself an outcast in the community despite your father's efforts to help you." She purses her lips, widens her eyes, lifts her brows high, giving me another stern look.

My brain feels like scrambled eggs, with her words all jumbled up, not making any sense. I was nervous and on edge the whole way here, and now I just feel numb. Allowing her to poke at me and giving her nothing.

"So, what do you have to say for yourself? You wanted to get rid of your dad, so you ran away, and when he rightfully came back for you after you dropped out of school, you put a bullet in his spleen and his head? Oh, and I almost forgot. We found these…" She fishes in her briefcase and pulls out some books. "These were hidden behind your Nancy Drew detective novels. How do you explain this atrocity?" She throws the books on the table causing a loud thud. I flinch. *"A Good Girl's Guide to Murder! How to Kill and Not be Killed? The Violence? How to Kill a Man and Get Away with It?* Well, *The Violence* was technically a novel my mom was reading, I found it in the attic with her sewing kit and her marble collection. Besides, I never even read any of those books. They were just there.

"I certainly have something to say to you, Missy! These are just the types of books that psychopathic murderers hide on their bookshelves! This is enough to convict you! This is enough for a jury to destroy you without a second thought!" She gives me a grinding look that makes me unsure if she's more upset with me because the books were hidden near the girl detective novels, and she takes offense to that, or she's sickened by the fact that I killed my dad. I mean, that someone killed my dad, not me, but she thinks that it was me. She like, really thinks that it's me. Maybe she's right, maybe I do have some hidden dark side to me. That could be true, but I know I am not responsible for murder!

I breathe deep and let out a long sigh. So, I missed my

birthday, and I was a witness to two murders in two nights. If I go ahead and tell Michaud here that I only saw my dad get murdered by my boyfriend and then my boyfriend was murdered by my boss the next night, she's not going to believe me. I don't think I really want to bring Claire into this. I'm not sure what her story will be, and she's right, I don't have a lot of people to back me up in this.

"I didn't kill anyone," I finally let out.

"Ms. Samson, please understand that you are looking at twenty years to life in prison, and if you admit to the crime, we can work out a deal. You can get ten years instead with parole and still be allowed to live a full enough life afterward."

"I DIDN'T KILL ANYONE!" I snap at her, frustrated by her trying to sound like she's helping me. Just coming into my work, accusing me of killing my dad, taking me away, probably lying about the calendar date. I've had enough of this already. I'm stuck here for a crime I didn't commit, and I have no one to help me. It's over.

"Okay, well you have been assigned a court-appointed attorney who will talk to you about working out a deal tomorrow. I'll bring you to your cell." She stands, with a disappointed look on her face, and I rise out of my chair. She cuffs me again and shows me to my cell.

We arrive, and Emma removes my cuffs. It's small, and there's a bunk bed with a tiny Hispanic woman lying on the bottom bunk reading a Vogue magazine. I turn around to see the bars sliding closed and Emma is already distant, walking down the hallway.

"You will be staying here in B pod." The Hispanic guard locks me in and leaves. Her boots clunking against the tile and her dangling keys clattering together from her belt loop. I turn around and look at the woman on the bed. Her black hair sprawled out like a web wrapping around the pillow and her face buried in her magazine. I just stand there looking at her, unaware of what I am doing and that as the minutes go by this girl will notice.

When she does, she turns her magazine over, showing me the page she's looking at. "Can you believe people are actually wearing shit like this?" She points to two women on the page dressed like a farmer's wife. I shake my head, indicating that I cannot believe it. "I mean fuck! This type of shit makes me not even mad that I'm in here and not out there." She folds a page, bookmarking her spot and sits up Indian style.

"Hi, I'm Marci." She smiles and wakes me up from an unconscious daze. Her lips are full and cracked and there's a gap between her front teeth. She's very thin and I'm guessing she's around forty. She lifts her hand to massage her neck, inclining it toward the ceiling, and I notice one arm is tattooed with roses and skulls of various sizes.

"You look like the summer camp counselor I stabbed in the hand with a pen when I was ten." I just stand there as she continues, "I was moved to a new foster family after that. It was good though because Darnel and Jeanette were wack. How did someone like you end up here anyway?" She scoots her body closer, her face set with intrigue and avidity as she wraps her arms around the bunk frame, the light revealing her green eyes that stand out against her chocolate skin. An inch-long scar sits on her left cheek, and it looks like someone had taken a knife across it before, but she's still pretty. Fine lines around her eyes indicate her older age, but her vibe seems playful like a child. She lights up like I'm about to tell a ghost story.

"I don't know why I'm here. I don't really understand."

"Aha, I get it. I don't really understand why I'm here either. One minute I'm hauling a safe from an art gallery into a pickup truck with my brothers, and the next thing I know some guy's running after us, creeps up behind one of my brothers, and has him in a chokehold, so I shoot him in the knee cap. Now I'm here… again." She laughs again until she notices I'm not going to laugh with her. "Seriously though, are you Okay?"

"I missed my birthday, and I'm being accused of my father's death. My boyfriend was the one who killed my father, and then my boss killed my boyfriend. I woke up dirty, went to work, and then I got arrested for something I didn't do."

"Damn, that is some crazy shit. What do you mean, you missed your birthday?"

"Supposedly, it was yesterday, and that would mean my boss killed my boyfriend who killed my dad two months ago. I woke up thinking it was the next day."

"Wow, I've heard a lot of stories in here, some about women killing their fathers. Hell, I've heard of some who have murdered their whole family." She laughs. "I mean there was this one girl who used to room in A pod, she stabbed her mother and father, then she took their bodies and hung them from a tree, and then she took her brother and…" She notices the look on my face, and that I'm not amused. "Never mind, that part isn't important. The point I am trying to make is that most people just pretend they're innocent, but you legit look innocent." She rakes her fingers through her hair and looks like she's trying to think of more to say. I just stare again for a moment. I feel the blood escaping my face and I'm lightheaded.

"My camp counselor's name was Leenah… so I'm gonna call you Leenah." She presses her lips together, points her arm out and forms a handgun with her index and thumb. Then she releases her lips making a popping sound before lowering her arm again.

"I think I'm going to lie down now." I point to the top bunk, and then step on to the ladder, pausing for a moment. "It was my eighteenth birthday that I missed. I was seventeen yesterday," I add on my way up the ladder. I collapse in my new bed, sinking my face into the pillow, my temples pounding, the hard mattress pressing firm against my body.

Chapter 12

There's a tug at my arm and then a push like a horse's hooves trampling down my back. Something clamps at my shoulders, then my side and my legs. Pushing and pulling at me gently at first and then escalating into a rough shake. I can't see anything, and I try to swat at whatever it is, pinching and picking at me, but nothing is there. Nothing that I can see. I think I hear a voice calling in the distance, faint at first, but then it gets louder. This thing, whatever it is, keeps brawling at me, and I think the voice is calling out something, but I can't make out what it is, and it's getting closer, but I can't focus on it with all this slapping and pinching, poking and pushing and smacking against me.

Suddenly, everything goes quiet, and the physical torture subsides. Off in the distance of this excruciatingly dark twilight zone, there's an hourglass shaped bottle. It appears to be just some ordinary bottle, until I recognize the smoke trail billowing out. The cough that escapes me is dramatic. My eyes squint, and then I clear the watery liquid seeping out from them. When I glance back up, I notice something strangely familiar and peculiar at the same time. The item reveals itself as the bottle from that show… *I Dream of Jeannie.* When the smoke simmers a bit, there's a profound billow of what appears to be a cloud, the sound of a woman coughing and clearing her throat is filtering through. Then, I hear her trampling from side to side, as if she has lost her balance.

There's a pause you can drive a truck through. The cloud

slowly vanishes. I am flabbergasted by what appears before me. It is Jeannie from the show, *I Dream of Jeannie!* I cannot believe it. It is Barbra Eden! Well, Jeannie, if she really exists before my eyes. She has the scarf hat, silver kitten heels, the crop top, and everything! Her ponytail is perfect enough to be a wig!

"I've come to hand you Jared's piece of writing," she says. There it is, Jared's play in her hands. After she forcefully places them in my hands, with a flip of her ponytail she turns back around like she has already completed her mission.

"Wait a minute!" I call out. She slowly turns back around.

"If you are really a Jeannie, that means I can wish myself out of this mess!" I shout, without a second thought at all. I am hopeful now that Jeannie has come to rescue me.

"I have not come to rescue you from jail. I'm not that kind of Jeannie." She shakes her head. I thought to myself for a moment. *What other kind of Jeannie is there?*

"I am a Jeannie of guidance and a Jeannie of unwant."

"Unwant?" I ask.

"Yes, I bring you things that you don't want to make you realize what you do want. And, well, I've done my duty for today." She steps back and crosses both of her forearms in front of her, blinking her long, fancy eyelashes. I know what this means. I have so many questions though. Before I could let out even the slightest sound, I open my mouth, and she's gone!

Then another voice emerges like a horn blowing in my ear. "Leenah! Leenah! Wake up! Leenah! Wake the fuck up!" Then I throw one last hand to the invisible, intrusive pest. My hand claps against the tender skin of my… cellmate!

"Jesus Christ, puta. Do you always sleep this heavily? And you're lucky I don't just knock your ass out again with my fist and really send you into next month." Marci caresses her cheek.

"I'm gonna let this one slide because you are new and for some reason, I think you're okay… for now, but Chica, you gotta get up. The guard called you five minutes ago to tell you that you have a visitor." She hops off the top bunk.

"I have a visitor? What time is it? How long have I been sleeping?" I kneed at my sheets and then palm my forehead. I search the area for Jared's story. I don't find it. Okay, so no Jeannie really appeared and handed me Jared's screenplay.

"Just a few hours." Marci massages her jaw, flips her hair behind her shoulder and plops down on a chair sitting in the corner. Her eyes are fierce, but watery and she clenches her fists. "Simone will be back in a minute to get you. That's what she said when you wouldn't wake up."

I sit upright on my bunk with my feet dangling over the edge. The socks they gave me are extra-large and slipping off. My toes stretching out into all the extra cloth. I massage my temples for a moment, wondering who my visitor could be. I pull at the heels of my socks, so my toes reach the end.

The guard has arrived back at my cell.

"You ready, Samson?" *Well, I suppose I have to be.* "Let's go," she says, rolling her eyes at me and slamming the cell door open. When I follow, she slams the cell door shut. She must not like her job very much. I can never understand why people stay at a job they don't like. It reminds me of my dad. He worked hard all the time, but he never enjoyed it. He was nice to everyone at work, but he came home and took his frustrations out on me. As we both turn to head down the walkway, another guard is screaming at a woman who is crying on the floor doing pushups. Her cell mates are all gathered to one side watching her as she struggles to continue. I guess the guards here can just take their frustrations out at work.

I walk down the hardwood floor of the hallway, avoiding eye contact with other cellmates as I pass, but I can feel the weight of their eyes on me as I focus on the heavy sound of the keys dangling together against Simone's upper thigh. We turn a sharp right around the corner then through an open door held open by a wooden wedge to the room with the round tables. Looking around, I notice every other table sits an inmate and either a couple or an individual sits across from them. I can hear a lot of mumbling and looks of worry and depression on their faces. As I maneuver through, I paste my eyes on some spiral red curls sweeping across gray cashmere on a tiny frame. Oh my God, of course it is her.

Simone escorts me over to the table that Claire is sitting at, and I'm reluctant to sit down on the stool across from her, but Simone blocks the straight way back to the doorway, and Claire has already noticed that I'm here. I pull a look at Simone displaying my annoyance. Maybe next time she won't wake me up for this. I sit down on the hard steal stool. Simone walks away. I am stuck sitting face to face with Claire, and my pulse quickens a bit as I wait for her to speak. She better have something good to say.

She shuffles through her purse a bit and applies some lip gloss with a hint of red coloring. I begin to feel jittery in my seat as I notice how calm and collected, she is even though she's guilty of murdering my lover, and she's sitting here in an actual prison. I'm shifting my body from one side to the other subtly, but noticeable. I try to pull myself together to match Claire's nonchalant and amenable body language, lace my fingers in front of me and look at her.

"So, I am happy that you are having some time to think about what you have done." She leans in closer and speaks more softly.

"I won't tell them about you murdering Jared. It doesn't seem necessary at this point, and I believe you have been through enough. You poor dear, are they feeding you enough in here?" she asks casually as if she's trying to sound like she's some type of hero doing me a favor.

Me murdering Jared? This is absurd. I have heard enough! This woman is an absolute psycho! I grind my teeth and surprisingly wait to hear what else she has to say.

"I've spoken to the counselor that you will be seeing. She seems nice, and I told her that you may just need some extra mental health support because everything that you have been through isn't your fault. You just broke down."

"What on earth are you talking about, Claire? You smashed a vase over Jared's head." I am angered at this ginger bitch, and my tolerance for this conversation is extremely low.

"Elise, I'm really worried about you. So is Julianna. She's been asking about you. Next time I will bring her with me, but I figured it may be too much for my first visit."

I glance over at the window, away from Claire's face. The warm sun is falling through the barbed wire screen holes. I see a walnut tree and freshly mowed grass, probably there to remind us that even though there is so much beauty on the outside, we are still trapped on the inside. A family rides by on their bicycles smiling. I turn my head back to Claire.

"You're going to get the help that you need, I made sure of it so don't work yourself up."

I blink a few times in disbelief. I begin to rise from my seat.

"I am the only one who can protect you here, Elise. The warden of this jail is a friend of mine, I created and designed the cake for his wedding."

I sit back down. *This is it. I am done for.* I think to myself, my head shifting downward, and then back up to Claire's arrogant face. Then out of the corner of my eye, I see Marci bolting toward me. She's like a woman in distress, frantically fleeing from a masked man in a horror movie. She links her arm with mine and puts her right hand up at Claire, signaling that this conversation is over.

"She's done here, she doesn't need to deal with this shit," Marci says. Claire's face fills with disgust.

"Who is this, Elise? Are you spending your time making friends in this ghastly, rotten, burden-infested dungeon?"

"Leenah, come on let's go." Marci is pulling me away as my eyes are still glued to Claire's face. Her frown turns into a smile, and it's giving me the creeps.

"Let's go, c'mon. Leenah wake up!" I lift my eyelids and turn my neck to see Marci's face hovering over me, and she's shaking my body. I prop myself up quickly, to the point where she leans back and must grab my arm and pull forward to prevent herself from falling backwards off the top bunk. I pull my sheet up and scooch back up against the wall in shock and confusion. Marci tilts her head. Wrinkling her forehead, she looks puzzled.

"Didn't you wake me up from my sleep for a visitor already? When did I fall back to sleep? Is Claire gone?"

"Girl, who the hell is Claire? And what are you talking about? You have been out since we last chatted, and it's dinner time. You haven't moved. I kinda thought you were dead."

"So, I've been sleeping this whole time?" I give Marci a deep, pressing stare into her eyes, like an inquiring wizard, looking deep for confirmation and truth. She gives me a sideways stare like I'm crazy. She nods her head yes.

"Yea girl, but let's go eat. I'm starving." She hops off the bed and I scratch my head then follow her. As I make my way off the top bunk, I hear the shuffle of papers stuffed between the mattress and the frame. Oh, God, it's Jared's story. There may be a mischievous Jeannie lurking around in here after all. Several guards are unlocking cells and patrolling the hallway as inmates scatter about, billowing down the hallway to have dinner. When we arrive in the mess hall, Marci links up with some more friends of hers on the way to the food line.

"Guys, this is my roomy, Leenah." The women just look me up and down simultaneously without introducing themselves. I'm starting to get used to being looked at like I don't really belong. Although I don't really think I belong here at all.

The women Marci hangs around with are mostly Hispanic, and they don't seem as friendly and welcoming as she was when we met in our cell. Marci grabs my arm, pulling me aside before we enter the line to grab our trays. A few guards roll carts out that have our trays of food underneath.

Marci leans in and tugs at me, indicating that she wants me to look at her face. She raises her eyebrows and looks up to me. I hadn't noticed before how petite Marci is.

"Where people sit here at lunch usually depends on race and crime." I scan the room, acknowledging the validity of her race statement. She points to the far-left side of the room.

"Those are the meth and cracks heads who are white." The druggies have messy, snarly looking hair, and I watch one give a smile to her friend, from a distance, I can see that she's missing a front tooth, and the rest are stained with obvious neglect.

"Over there." She shifts her finger over. "Those are black people who supposedly only made one mistake and are claiming to be innocent." She looks up at me again. "Some of them have set something on fire because they have been pushed over the edge. Us colored people grow up having to keep things inside and not show weakness." She puts her arm back down and chin-gestures to another table of black women.

"Those are repeated offenders. They've been here before, but they don't hang around the other black Chicas because they don't believe in playing the victim, so they don't trust them." She then nods her head toward the table on the left. I look over at the tables with Hispanics and other races.

"Us Hispanics stick together. White Chicas sit with us most of the time unless they would rather sit with the crack heads. Something about being mistreated by their white counterparts. We had a child psychologist in here, and she taught us all about transference and projection, and how if you are discriminated against by your race you will try to blend in with other races."

"Oh, I didn't know that, but that makes sense."

"Ya, she was chill. She had us counseling the counselors. *Haha!*" She slaps her hand on her thigh and she's full of laughter. "They didn't like that very much."

"What ended up happening to her?"

"Well, she was here because one of her clients was being abused by her dad. She, the child, kept coming into her office crying and not wanting to go over there. The mom had a court order and was legally obligated to send her there. He was also a heroin addict, so Keri-that was her name, went undercover and bought heroin from a drug dealer, laced it with rat poisoning, and started going to a bar she heard he was a regular at. She got flirty with him and eventually gave him the heroin that killed him."

"Oh my God, didn't he know who the child's therapist was?" Curiosity consumes me.

"He never got to meet the therapist. The little girl was too afraid to talk about having one when she was over there." Marci grabs me again by the arm, gesturing me to come and get a tray of food.

"So, do you know what happened next with the therapist? Did they have evidence it was her?" I pull my tray of food out. There's a carton of one percent milk, a mixed fruit cup, and a warming container holding the main meal. We start walking over to the table. Marci plops onto her stool and smacks her tray on the table. I sit down on an empty seat across from her, still listening attentively, eager to hear what happened to the therapist.

"So, she killed the father, and the case was open for months until the drug dealer was caught dealing. The cops wanted a bigger fish to bag so her name was mentioned." She shoves some broccoli into her mouth and moves it to one side making her cheek bulge. "And well, she had intent to kill so she was brought here. They transferred her out a couple of months ago, and God only knows where." She opens her milk, and I open mine and take a sip. That therapist sounds like a hero to me for what she did for that little girl. The system seems so broken, and there needs to be more heroes like that in this world.

"I think they were also mad that she was teaching us so much. We were giving the counselors here a taste of their own medicine, and when she left, they got all their control and power back." She takes a big gulp of milk.

All around us I hear rowdy talk and mumbling, the sound of trays shuffling around on the tables, and beige jumpsuits maneuvering around making the spacious cafeteria like a pen of uniformed children. Marci slams her milk down.

"She did all of that for her client?" I think of Jared and all he tried to do for me.

My heart fills with sorrow because I miss him so much. I think of how he wouldn't give up on me and the threatening look that exposed his dark side and filled his gorgeous blue eyes with fire when he pulled the trigger to save me from my dad.

"Yep! And she didn't have to – going undercover and shit for nothing in return. Don't expect that from anyone in this bitch." She flips her hair, so it falls behind her shoulders, and I open the cover of my warming plate, revealing a large slice of lasagna and some steamed broccoli. The ricotta cheese is falling out from the sides, and some burnt cheese encrusts the edges. I'm starved, so I dig right in.

"Janaiya, you remember Keri, right?" Marci elbows the Latina girl with short curly hair sitting next to her.

"Hell yeah I do. That bitch was fine as hell," she replies before stuffing her face with ground beef and melted cheese. "I'm about to take Alejandro's keys from his key ring, stab him right in the eye, and have them send me off to wherever she's at." She throws her thumb over her shoulder to point to a guard standing in the far-right corner of the room, holding his hands together in front of his pelvis. He has black hair and caramel skin. His facial expression says that he's ready to pounce on anyone who tries to cross him, like a lion guarding his throne and protecting his reputation as king.

A tray of food smacks against my shoulder blade as I turn my neck to find out why and I wipe my hands through my ponytail and pull out Jell-O chunks. There's a tall lanky girl with a buzz cut hovering over another girl, picking up the remains of her dinner tray. Marci reaches for my hand. "That's Denise, she's a bully here, but we all feel sorry for her because she has a peanut allergy. We just let her belittle us and smack food trays out of our hands because we can literally take her out with a bag of trail mix. She takes her frustrations out on us. She's been here a while."

"You guys just let her run your life because you feel bad

about her food allergy?" Suddenly the table is full of women forcing their eyes to wander all over the place, anything to avoid contact with my question. Not sure if they are embarrassed or just don't want to respond to someone reiterating what Marci had just explained to me.

"She once poured her whole chocolate milk carton over my head. For no apparent reason at all. Then she just stomped away furiously and as if I was the bad guy in the scenario. I'm Ava by the way." The pretty girl with short blonde curls next to me introduces herself. She holds her hand out, and I shake it. It is warm and a little clammy. I give a subtle smile, but I'm still in disbelief that these females who seem like they would destroy anyone who crossed them, would let someone control them just because they're allergic to something so mundane like peanuts. This particular phenomenon is mind-bending.

Chapter 13

I open my eyes to a pale-yellow ceiling, barely lit by the hallway light. I can feel the air flowing through the vents and it's cold. I have the sheets ruffled up, covering my mouth and nose. I hear a guard's boots bumping against the floor like duct tape pressing against the tile and then being ripped up again several times. It's drowning out the sound of conversations between other inmates in their cells. Below me, I can hear the crinkling sound of Marci turning the page of one of her magazines. I don't remember having a dream, but I feel relieved that I didn't have a nightmare. I'm still in jail, and now my only fear is the unknown.

    I take a deep breath in, hold it for a couple of seconds, and take a long breath out. I relax my back against the wall, sitting upright in my bunk. The skin on my hands and face feel dry from the Johnson's baby soap they give us to wash up with. My hair is barely combable, dressed in snarls and dead ends.

    Simone comes to tell me that my attorney is waiting for me in the interrogation room. The same gloomy room where Michaud accused me of murder. My pulse quickens, and I really do feel unsure about an attorney representing me for a crime I didn't commit. This is one big murder mystery where I am the only one who has cracked the case. Everyone else just needs to catch up.

    I follow Simone. My body is filled with dread and hopelessness. The taste of chocolate chip muffin, home fries, and bitter coffee still lingering in my mouth. Dismay is clutching at my throat. I wonder if I should just go with the flow and comply with whatever these people want me to do.

We turn the corner and both of our heads peer through the window. I see a dark-haired man wearing a navy-blue suit flipping through pages on top of a manila folder. Not the manila folder filled with 'paperwork.' I hate those stupid folders filled with statements given by other people who don't even know me that well. I barely speak to anyone, how can there be a stack full of papers about me? Simone puts her hand on the door latch.

"Court appointed attorneys are usually interns, but you are pretty lucky to have this one because he's had a lot of training due to his dad also being an attorney for many years. Do you have any questions before you meet him?"

I shake my head 'no' and she lets me in the room. I look at the man sitting down in his chair, and he turns to look back at me. Suddenly I feel as if I have just been shocked by a defibrillator! The face on top of this suit and fiery orange precisely knotted tie... is... Jared! It is as if a handsome prince awakened me. Oh, how I longed for this moment since I woke up in my bed, filthy and confused. Oh no, what about his zombie raccoon screenplay? It's still at The Cake House! I'll just explain that to him so he can go retrieve it since he's the one who isn't trapped.

I cannot believe my eyes. My throat is a little scratchy and my heart still thumping. My body is probably trying to catch up with this news that Jared is right here in front of me.

He pulls the paperwork together and straightens it out, using the table as a base. The chair screeches again and the hair on my arms spike up as he eases up out of his chair, reaching his hand out to greet me. My eyes scan him up and down.

"Nice to meet you, Elise. I've been reading up on some

paperwork about your case here." He slightly shifts his body to the side and points to the file. I glance down at the file, but then my eyes drift right back to his ocean eyes. They're filled with innocence today, and wow, we have so much to catch up on, starting with... he is here right now, visiting me in prison. Oh well, I guess what matters most is that I have the same butterflies in the stomach feeling I got the first time I laid eyes on this gorgeous man. His parents deserve an award for creating such a beautiful creature.

His goatee is shaved, and he smells like an expensive aftershave. I also get a whiff of cologne – also probably pretty expensive.

"Jared?"

He raises one eyebrow, his arm still held out awkwardly, but he doesn't seem to mind. I place my hand in his.

"Yes, I see they already told you my name. I'm your attorney." His smile is bright – very white like he could be on a crest with whitening toothpaste commercial – with an added sparkling star photoshopped in at the edge of his mouth.

"But how did you...?"

"Here, come sit down, and I will go over my role as your attorney."

"But Jared... it's me... Elise."

"Yes, you are Elise." He pats both his hands on his chest. "And I'm your attorney... Jared." He gives me a sideways look like I may be crazy, but it's okay because he's used to this behavior.

Wait a minute, let's rewind. I saw Jared lying on the floor with a seriously disgusting gash on his head. I checked for a pulse. I checked for signs of breathing. He was dead. And he sure as hell didn't want to be an attorney. *What is going on here?*

"Jared, it's Elise. You don't remember me?" He nods his head almost too slowly.

"Yes, I understand that you are Elise. We established this. I am Jared." He pats his hands to his chest again, and I realize that he really doesn't remember me. We could end up repeating this same conversation over and over again if I continue. I can already feel the tears coming on like an emerging river pushing through stones to create a waterfall.

Jared – the one person who wanted me to make the best of my life, believed in me, and understood my pain – is now just a face. Like a replica of the babe I knew, and an addition to this nightmare of untruth and confusion.

I subtly pinch my forearm just to be sure I'm not sleeping, and the pain sends a teardrop out of one eye. I swipe my knuckle immediately under the tear duct and use my other hand to wipe my cheek. I rake my fingers through my hair, and then I move some hair behind my ears. I straighten myself out, making the tear less noticeable, and I clear my throat.

Jared glances down at my paperwork, and he points the tip of his pen at what is written at the top of the page.

"So, when was the last time you saw your dad?" I blink a few times and gaze into his dreamy eyes as he waits for an answer. *The last time I saw my dad was when you shot him between the eyes, Jared!*

"I don't remember." I cross my arms. My answer feels suitable for this conversation. My eyes shift toward the tiny dust particles floating above his perfectly gelled hair. I liked his hair before he came back from the dead, or whatever happened. It was all over the place at times, ignoring perfection completely. It was beautiful.

He licks his lips and leans back, waiting to see if I'm going to add more or change my answer. When he realizes he's waiting for nothing, he shifts his eyes back to the paper, jots down my short answer, and continues tapping the end of the pen to the table.

"Do you know where your mom is?" he asks, and I feel my heart being tugged at, like a bear's paw at my ventricles and pinning its claws in just enough to spark a massively painful reaction. I let my tears fall out this time, and he reaches for a box of tissues at the end of the table and hands them over to me. He looks at me sympathetically, which makes it even harder to keep crying.

"My mom is in heaven," I say, continuously wiping tears from my cheeks. Well at least I hope she is, and I hope my dad is receiving whatever treatment he deserves on the other side that correlates with the spiritual force that he's been serving here on earth.

The look on Jared's face transforms into a more serious one. One that makes me curious.

"How would you describe your relationship with your dad?"

"You already know the answer to this, Jared. Why are you acting like you don't?"

"Would you say that when you do something wrong that would result in appropriate punishment, he corrects you and guides you in the right direction?"

"*Grrr*... you're telling me you don't remember asking me out at The Cake House? Or our plans to move to Los Angeles, where you can make your weird zombie raccoon story into a movie?" I lean forward and purse my lips, giving him a dead stare.

"Does your father set rules about pocket money?" he yells.

What the heck? Pocket money? What does that have to do

with murder? Are we even in the same room right now? Having the same conversation?

His mouth drops a bit, and yet another puzzled look takes over his perfect face. I place my fist under my chin and look deep into his eyes – searching for answers. He glances back down, ignoring my questions.

"So, it says here that you ran away from your dad, and he came looking for you? That sounds like something a dad would normally do, right?"

I feel my eyes roll. I can't possibly take him seriously any more.

"Jared, you don't even want to be an attorney. What are you even doing here? You want to be a writer. You finished a story that you were so excited about."

He closes the folder and breathes in a deep breath, letting out an exasperated sigh.

"I see we are not getting anywhere today. Would you like a notebook and pencil? Is that what you are trying to ask for?" he asks. I let out my own exasperated sigh. I'm so frustrated right now I could just lift this whole table and throw it on top of Jared. It's not like things could get any worse for me.

"Fine," I reply.

"Yeah, that shouldn't be a problem. I can get you that." The folder remains closed, and he continues to tap his pen on the folder.

"My role as your attorney is to help represent you and convince the jury that you are innocent. Right now, there seems to be enough evidence that you would kill your father due to the fact that you had a terrible relationship with him and wanted to get away from him." He drops his pen and rubs his palms together.

"Or…" He pauses and props both hands outward, palms facing up. "We could work out a deal, where you admit to killing your dad, and you will face the minimum of ten years."

I rub my palms together and shrug my shoulders.

"Well, I will check up with you again about that at a different time," he says after realizing a shrug is all he is going to get at this time.

He opens the manila folder and pulls out a piece of paper.

"Here, if no one can provide you with money for commissary – to get more necessities while in jail – this is an application for government assistance. You can hand it in to me next time we talk."

I take the paper. I barely even remember everything we just talked about. Probably went right through me again, a familiar feeling, hitting me like a bus that can't seem to slam on its breaks in time.

We conclude our conversation, and he assures me that a guard will be bringing me a notebook and pencil. I thank him even though I really want to knock some sense into his pretty boy, big shot lawyer intern head of his. *Where is the werewolf, lying to his parents about college, adventure seeking, takes nobody's crap, living life on the edge, spontaneous boy I met at The Cake House?*

Chapter 14

I feel mentally isolated from everyone in this jail, but I suppose one of the perks is that we get to go outside for an hour each day. I haven't gotten any commissary money yet, but Marci let me borrow a knitted scarf. Marci has a lot of stuff in our cell. Flip flops for the shower, shampoo with shea butter, and she can get Coca-Cola.

"I have tons of clothing that was donated to me when I was in foster care, and I kept a lot of things throughout the years."

"Thanks. I have a government application so I can receive necessities too."

It's cold out here, and while most of the women are socializing, taking a walk in the courtyard, coloring, or playing games, I'm like an invisible shadow sitting aside watching. They seem to have no worries at all. They know what they've done. They are making the best of their time here.

I cross my legs, close my eyes, and face directly up at the afternoon sun. My journal is in my hand, and there is more to read in Jared's story. Maybe if he had the chance to read it now his memory would come back. As my attorney he could get me out of here if he could only remember. We could finish our journey to Hollywood and put his story on the big screen. I wonder why I'm so electrified by this now. I wasn't in the other universe.

I thought Jared was insane when he first told me about the zombies who turn into pesty raccoons during the day. I thought it would make more sense for him to become a lawyer, but his creativity is on to something. *Why did Jeannie want me to read it so much if Jared is not the same person?* Instead, he's falsely convicting me (even though he's supposed to be on my side). I'm the crazy one now, in this world some monster created. If I ever write a story about my life, which I should. I am going to call it Monster World. Yes, and everyone in my life can be a part of my story. Jared has become inspirational, yet another flash of lightning down my spine.

Damn it, why did I think Jared's goal was ridiculous. I feel like this is all my fault! It is all my fault. If I had just stayed with him that night after he murdered my dad everything would be different, and he wouldn't be stuck being a lawyer! We could tell stories together.

A ping pong ball rolls over to my foot. I kick it back to the players. When I look up, I catch eyes with a guard who notices that I'm all alone and walks over to me. A black squirrel dashes through the courtyard and into a bush set against the building. My foot taps on the cement at the same pace as my pen taps against my journal.

"What ya writing in that notebook you got there?" he asks, shooting me a friendly smile. "My name's James, by the way."

"Elise," I say. "Nothing yet," I reply. I open the notebook to reveal the blank pages. The only purpose this notebook has served so far is a place to doodle, which is clear when you look inside the front cover.

I close the book and almost instantaneously I think of an idea. What if I write to Jared about how I felt when we met and show it to him? There's a good chance he will remember everything! Either that or I show him *Long Live the Troubled*. Which would obviously uncover even more madness containing a Jeannie in a bottle who brought it here. Plus, they have a whole list of things I brought in here… nothing, so if he finds out I have the screenplay he wrote and reply that a Jeannie brought it to me, it will out the inevitable illusion that I am absolutely insane! Nobody will believe a thing I say. I will just write about our meeting for now and test the waters.

"Well, I'm sure you will think of something. If you need any help with anything, or if you have any questions while you are here, let me know."

"Thank you," I say. He turns around and walks over to the women playing UNO and checks in with them.

I reopen the notebook and press the eraser of my pencil to my lips.

"Hmm… to remember how I felt when I first laid eyes on Jared," I whisper softly to myself.

Can I have a slice of the cake behind you?

Memories of the time we spent together creep to the surface of my mind. From the day we met, to when he brought me to a party to meet his friends, to every date, and every kiss. Most importantly, I remember how he truly showed that he cared for me. He saw me in his future and in his dreams. My eyes begin to water.

"All right, time to clean up and get back to your cells!" James shouts. He links his thumbs through his belt loops, and he walks around to make sure everyone is tidying up, and we head back inside. Upon arrival to my luxurious imprisonment closet, I once again pick up Jared's pile of papers, worth whatever HBO would be willing to give it.

Oakland gallops through the desert-like town, and he stops at Soup's On, a café with incredible taste. They feed him, the workers. He orders a turkey, bacon, lettuce, tomato, and provolone cheese sandwich on a French Baguette with a mango tango smoothie. Next, he's on his way; if he is in control, he will move along like the others.

At this next organization, he's enriched with a Firey fury. An iceberg freezes his nervous system at the same time as a flame ignites from his groin. The Boys and Girls Club. In another life, he was mistreated there. He approaches, as he watches the children playing around in the yard with an ice cream truck there, delivering goodies. Yes, he remembers when he got smacked with an M&M cookie ice cream. The coordinating staff said it was okay for this to be done to me. Oakland is going to make a scene this time. He's going to make them give him his free ice cream.

My eyes grow tired. Jared's story must have slipped down my arm and drifted down onto the floor. Before I can drift off into a deep sleep, Jeannie is hovering over me inquisitively, as my heart and eyelids long for closing. She grins.

"How is it going so far? You are reading?"

"Yes, but now I am tired. Wait a second..." I peak my head down at the bottom bunk to see if Marci is there to witness this Jeannie. There's no Marci, just an unmade bed with ruffled up sheets. I sigh very loudly, blowing breath like a strong wind through Jeannie's perfect bangs. They fall right back down into place.

She's wearing a dimpled smile and looks eager. She climbs up the ladder and sits down next to me with her knuckles planted under her chin.

"What do you think of Jared's story?" she asks. Why on earth does she care so much about Jared's story? When there's a silence, she breaks it. She snaps her fingers, and a black squirrel appears in my cell. The creature has a stumpy looking tail, and he's chunky. Jeannie hops off the bunk and I follow. The squirrel is so cute, and he seems to love me. His eyes are very large, brown like the mudholes you find treasure in if you look into them and the snake doesn't bite you first. He rubs up against my jumpsuit like a kitty cat. I'm standing there with a bag of peanuts.

I toss the bag over to Jeannie and at lightning speed she tosses it right back to me. I hear the clanking sound of beltloop keys coming from down the hallway. Someone is going to find out that I have been feeding a squirrel, and I haven't been! Jeannie eyeballs where the sound is coming from and shifts her glance back at me. My face feels hot.

"They are going to wonder why there is a squirrel in your cell," Jeannie states right before she crosses her arms. The sound of clanking keys grows louder, and it feels like caged bats are fluttering around in my ribcage. It seems like the sound is growing closer and closer by the second.

"No, Jeannie, you have to get out of here, and take this bag and the squirrel with you!" I shove the bag back into her hands and push her toward the corner of the cell. Suddenly, she and the squirrel vanish into thin air, and I crash into the corner as the bottle drops on my head.

"Is everything okay over here?" James flashes a flashlight in my cell. He doesn't have to use a flashlight; it's already lit up enough in here. I am relieved because everything is actually okay.

"Yeah, I just tripped," I reply. "Everything's fine, I'm just tired. I feel dizzy from my medication, so I think I am going to lie down now." He nods and walks away.

Finally, Jeannie's out of the way, but I can't just have her showing up out of nowhere whenever she wants! It was interesting the first time. Now she can just get me in trouble!

As I make my way up to my bunk, my head sinks down into my pillow, eyes still wide open as I wait for Marci's return before I close them again.

In a few minutes, I'm scheduled to meet with Jared again. A bunch of us women are in the television room. I have no idea what Jared is going to say. This could go really well... or really bad. I shove my fingers into my hair. Then I fix it up – intently trying to look pleasant.

The other inmates are watching *Law and Order*. All I see in the show are people crying and a lot of court and judgement. I'm filling out the application for monthly payments for commissary. I started to write my story called, *Monster World*, and it began when I was born, I was stolen from the hospital by a woman who wore a man suit to disguise herself. She could pull off her skin and replace it with the skin of an evil man monster! This woman had been in the mental institution several times, but she was actively taking her medication. No one had noticed there was anything wrong except for the fact that there were two people living in her home, but only one was seen at a time. Then suddenly, a child was 'born.'

As I grew older... in the story, I knew about my 'mother' and the man suit, and it was explained to me that she must disguise herself as a man because men get away with more in society. I did not question anything except for the fact that I was homeschooled by a robot. This robot took care of me while my mother-father was at work. The robot was programmed to teach me a limited amount of literature and math. This was no ordinary robot; you could not just destroy the mechanical device with water. And my robot teacher-nanny would tie my hands behind my back and drip drops of water between my eyes if I were noncompliant with student-like tasks.

That's all I wrote so far before I realized I was probably going to finish a whole novel in a week before writing what I was supposed to write to Jared. I wrote a little bit about my time with Jared before he died... and came back.

I peek through the window, and I notice Jared is here. I'm filled with both nervousness and anticipation. I want him to see what I wrote so far... and I also don't.

When I met you at The Cake House, my first thought was that you were just another hottie, but then you asked for a piece of my cake that was caving in with cracks all over it. Butterflies instantly took charge of my stomach when I looked into your eyes. It gave me such a warm feeling as if you ignited a fire within me.

You continued to come to the Cake House to see me, and I kept falling for you every time. Falling like the last of the orange and red leaves on the verge of the coldest season. First you were there to pick up a cake for a party, and then you were there to treat yourself. You were treating me too when you came to my line. The beautiful feeling would come to me every time you were present. I loved the way I would melt in your arms when we kissed, or when I could hear your heartbeat when you held me. It was a magical feeling.

I look back up from my notebook, and I see him chatting with an attractive female. I'm assuming she works here because she's wearing a lanyard and not a jumpsuit. She has beautiful blonde hair with pink highlights. I look down at my dead ends.

"Who is that woman in the window?" I elbow a girl named Jolene sitting next to me.

"Oh, that's Gina. She runs our groups. We probably have some group in a few minutes about suicide or mental illness."

I turn my head back to the window. I watch Jared give her a

kiss on the cheek and place lose strands of hair behind her ears. *What? He gave her a kiss?* He is caressing her stylish locks in an intimate encounter. Oh no, this really is my worst nightmare. I can't show Jared what I wrote for him now! My heart is shattering, and the pieces are falling one by one into the rabbit hole. Jared is my one chance at freedom, at love, and it's already too late. How can an inmate about to be on trial for murder compete with someone who runs groups for the fallen and clearly has it all together?

It looks like she is his girlfriend, his intimate, passionate lover. Well, that was fast. He wanted me to be his girlfriend so we can run away across the country to make a movie just a week ago. I shut the notebook and bite the inside of my cheek. I don't see how this could get any worse.

Jared strolls into the lounge area as if nothing happened. He tells me that we can meet right after I have a group session with Gina. We are expected to attend the groups in this room, I guess. He smiles at me, but I am certainly not pleased. I smile back at him, pretending to be content with the situation, but I am full of so much jealousy, I am about to explode.

Now I have to go to a group session with his girlfriend? I can't believe he is crushing my soul like this. He might as well just rip my heart out with daggering claws and flush it down the toilet. He walks out the door without a care in the world, and I'm biting down hard on my lip. My teeth start grinding together uncontrollably. An unsettling feeling flows through me as he vanishes in the doorway.

Gina barges in, picks up the remote, and shuts off the television right in the middle of an episode. She hands out an article about mental illness. I look around at the small group of women in the room, all from pod B.

"Hi, I'm Gina," she says. "As you all may know, people who end up serving jail time typically have some type of mental illness. Jail is a place where you are kept away from the rest of society until you have learned your lesson about any damage you have done. It is supposed to be a punishment, but I like to call it a time of healing." She smiles delightfully as if we are all supposed to be moved by her charisma. After handing everyone an article she sits down across from the couch that I am sitting on with Jolene and two other women.

This woman has no idea. Accusing me of having a mental illness? She's the one with a guy who thinks he can write a zombie raccoon movie and turn it into a movie in Hollywood.

Oh, but I love him too. I open my notebook and flip through the pages of *Monster World*. I doodle a star next to the sentence where I left off. I saw one girl with a gel pen, and I am hoping they have them in commissary, and I can get some when my government assistance comes in. Gina clears her throat loudly, and I hurry to close my notebook.

Gina is pretty and she's in the same career field as Jared. They do make a cute couple. I can't deny that. She's beautiful actually. Her eyes are a little spaced apart, but it doesn't look like she has to do much to her hair to keep it looking shiny and silky, with waves on the ends.

She's dressed casually with a peony pink sweater, khakis, and matching Keds. She's wearing fancy glasses with large clear frames. Her lips are glossy, and through the wide lenses of her glasses, I can see that her eyelashes are curled.

She asks us to go around the room and read two paragraphs each from the article. Then we have a little discussion.

"It's important for you all to understand your mental illness while you are in here and when you leave here. Ask yourself what triggers you to make such destructive decisions. Would anyone like to share their thoughts about this topic with the rest of the group?"

"I have a question," Jolene chimes in.

"Ask away," Gina says.

"I feel like I was thrown in here for external reasons. Like I was really pushed over the edge before I had a breakdown and stole a bunch of jewelry. Why do I feel like I was pushed over the edge?" She starts crying a little and a few whispers of crosstalk float through the room.

"That's a very good question, would anyone in the group like to answer Jolene's question."

The room goes silent.

"'Cause the world is shit, that's why," a girl sitting next to Marci replies.

"We have control over who we choose to have in our lives," Gina replies. "The people who set off our triggers either teach us who to keep in our circle, or what we need to work on for ourselves," Gina says, glancing at everyone in the room.

"Would anyone like to share any of their coping skills?" She looks around the room again and it's silent. "Nobody has any coping skills? Okay, how about this, we go around the room and each name a skill we want to learn. I'll go first. I would like to learn how to play the piano." She looks over at Marci, who is sitting to her right. Marci rolls her eyes and leans back on the sofa.

"I guess I would like to learn how to draw," she says.

"I would like to learn how to paint," Janaiya says.

When it's my turn, I state that I would like to learn creative writing.

"Okay, you all did a great job-sharing what skills you would like to learn." Gina crosses her legs. She's not only pretty, but she's nice, and everyone is on their best behavior in front of her.

"Learning something new is a big step toward recovery because it helps us with our self-confidence. When we develop a good sense of self-confidence, we make better decisions about who we allow in our lives and what we deserve."

Gina scans the room full of quiet women.

"Does anyone have anything they would like to add to our discussion for today?"

I raise my hand shyly.

"My dad was murdered. My boyfriend shot him." I pause and think for a moment about what I am saying out loud. "I watched my boyfriend shoot him because he attacked me." I look around at the wide eyes filled with interest. I continue with my story. "My boyfriend came to my place of employment to talk, convince me to run away with him, or whatever. My boss smashed a vase over his head and killed him." I slowly breathe in through my nose. "And now I'm here. My boyfriend is also here, but he doesn't know he's my boyfriend."

I watch as the mouths of these listening women drop open, looking amazed by my factual ghost story. I look over at Gina. Her face is filled with anger, and she huffs and puffs like the wolf in the story of the three little pigs.

"You lying bitch! You killed your own father because you are a selfish, heartless little shit! And now I'm going to kill you!" She bolts toward me, grabbing my neck with both hands and squeezing tightly, her teeth grinding together. I grab her arms, trying to struggle out of her grasp, and I gasp for air. I can't breathe. My feet are kicking, and my hands are swatting. When I lose the strength to keep fighting, I feel myself sliding down into my chair and everything looks blurry before my eyes close shut.

"Okay, since nobody has any questions, I guess that

concludes our group for today," Gina says. The group rises from their chairs. I touch my neck and my face, watching the other inmates leave the room.

"Are you okay?" Gina asks.

"Oh… ya, I'm fine." I ease up from my seat and hurry out of the room, wiping my sweaty palms on my jumpsuit. My head feels dizzy. I should probably tell someone about my low blood sugar that I've been ignoring.

As I walk down the hallway, a bald man in a white lab coat approaches me.

"Are you…" He glances down at his clipboard. "Elise Samson?"

"Yep, that's me," I say in a careless tone as I roll my eyes.

"Oh, good. I'm glad I found you. I asked your cell mate where you were and she told me her roommate's name is Leenah, so I got a little confused."

"It is! I mean, they're both my names." He shoots me a puzzled look and then continues.

"I'm Dr. Davis. I am the psychiatrist here at Ludlow Jail. I am responsible for prescribing medication to you while you are in here."

He flashes an ear-to-ear grin as if I am supposed to be amused, flattered to find out what type of illness got me placed in here.

"Do you have a few minutes to talk in my office?"

"Sorry, I have a meeting with my attorney right now." I pat him on the arm gently and proceed down the hallway before he has time to say anything else. I walk toward the room where I will be meeting with Jared. I wonder if that's the guy I should talk to about my blood sugar issue. Nah, maybe I should just keep that to myself so that nobody messes with my meals. The last thing I need right now is dessert removed from my plate.

Chapter 15

I step into the interrogation room where Jared is waiting to speak to me again. James closes the door behind me, and I sit down on the chair across from Jared and hand him my application for assistance. Jared is dressed in a beige suit today which matches my jumpsuit. His tie is maroon. Glasses with black rectangular frames are set over his eyes, and his shoes are shiny and polished. My eyes search the top of his forehead for a scar.

"Um, is there something on my head?" He rakes his fingers through his hair.

"Oh no, I was just checking if you had any dandruff."

His eyebrows furrow. *I'm just checking to see if you have any dandruff? Really Elise?*

"I have some good news and some bad news for you, Elise." He picks up a piece of paper and draws it closer to his face. My pulse quickens because there is bad news and I have an ominous feeling that the good news won't help much.

Jared killed my dad and he's sitting here representing me for my false conviction. He fishes through his briefcase and pulls out a handgun in a plastic bag. He plops it on the table. His expression is difficult to read, but this is certainly the gun he used to shoot my dad.

"Do you know what this is?" he asks. His fatherly tone is amplified.

"A gun," I say plainly.

"This is a Glock 19 handgun." He pierces his werewolf eyes

into mine, reaching my soul. "You can only buy a Glock 19 handgun from a licensed gun store. If a person wanted to casually walk into a store and buy a gun like this, they too would need to be licensed to carry. Now where would a seventeen-year-old, because you were seventeen at the time, get a hold of a Glock 19 handgun?" He leans in almost too dramatically. Then he points to the gun. It looks as if he wants me to be innocent, because the facts don't add up, but he's forced to believe the other side. I shrug my shoulders.

"This was found on a search at Lake Congomond." He looks down in a dispiriting way. Then he slowly glances up again. "Elise, your fingerprints were found on this handgun." He digs back into his briefcase and pulls out a picture that was taken that night. It was me dragging my dad's body into the lake… ALONE! Who would take a picture of that? There is also a turquoise impala in the picture. Claire drives a turquoise impala!

"Evidently, it is you who murdered your father, Elise." His voice breaks out into a disheartening tone.

"I wasn't the one who killed my dad, and I definitely did not dispose of his body alone!"

"I do not understand why you do not remember shooting your dad and hauling him into the lake." He scratches his head. "This just seems to me like something that a person would remember."

"I know, Jared! Maybe it's the same reason you don't remember shooting my dad and dragging him into the lake!" I yell.

I cross my arms. My eyes are glued on the pictures. Then I spare a cautious glance back up at him. His jaw drops at my yelping. He leans forward again.

"Listen, I can have you committed to a mental hospital if you continue to tell me that I killed your dad. I do understand that you are going through a lot, but what you keep telling me is not going to help your case. We can work out a deal – the ten-year deal still stands. Your court hearing is next week." He's talking to me like a parent frustrated with a child. He's disappointed in me, and he really wants me to explain why I committed this crime.

What am I going to do? There's clear evidence that I killed my dad, and I really didn't. Nothing has ever made less sense to me. I shake my head and think to myself, *what the heck is the good news?*

Later that day, everyone from B Pod is brought into a room that horrifyingly resembles a classroom. Long tables with chairs spread out, reminding me of eighth grade science with Mr. Galligan. Gina's there, and she tells us we are going to be making vision boards. There are poster boards, markers, stickers, inspirational phrases all cut out, magazines, and glue sticks set up for us to grab while walking into the room.

Gina has on a Tulu skirt with a velvet top and lace sleeves. Her hair is pulled back in a ponytail, a fluffy ponytail with no lose ends. Ugh, and I'm in a beige jumpsuit. She probably enjoys flaunting her fashionable, flawless self and attire around the detention center. I, like the rest of the pod, pick out some artistry to place on my board, then I sit down and stare at the wall for a few minutes. Jolene, who is sitting right beside me is already hard at work.

I can see her pencil moving rapidly like she's an architect drawing out designs. I sneak a peek and gather that she really is drawing everything out herself.

"Can I see what your vision board looks like?" I ask. She moves her arm out of the way without hesitation. She looks like she was waiting for me to ask.

"Over here, I have my sister, who is being stabbed by two men who broke into her apartment in the middle of the night, when she fell asleep on the couch. See here how the cushions are blood-stained, and the blood keeps gushing out of her as they keep stabbing at her?" She points everything out to me. The two men with their knives raised in the air, the poor woman bleeding, wounded in her sleep. I feel nauseous, a pain in the pit of my stomach, as Jolene goes on to describe the next picture.

"And over here." She slides her pointer finger over to another drawing on her board. "This is my daughter taking care of my ex because he can't take care of her. Those dirty needles over there on the table off to the corner are his because he's a chronic heroin user. Look at how my daughter is feeding him the last of the food on her plate, they are both crouched over, and her face is green." She describes all of this to me with a straight face. I want to throw up and cry.

"*Eergh*... yeah... I see it... you don't have to show me any more." I shift my body to the other side, reaching for some stickers and magazine cut-outs of pet rabbits, gardens, a plate of tofu salad with vibrant veggies, and the Eiffel tower. I feel very sick. Gina stands up from her chair in the front of the room. She raises her hand, trying to grab everyone's attention.

"Would anyone like to share their vision board with the rest of the pod?" she asks. There's an eerie silence that the legs of a daddy longlegs spider walking across the floor could break. Jolene raises her hand. I cringe as I stick a fox sticker onto my board only a third of the way done. I can hear Gina gulp as she eyeballs her graphic vision board. With the tap of a finger to her apple watch, she takes her offer to share vision boards back.

"Oh, I must have lost track of time. It's time for us to clean up and return to our cells. Maybe we can share our boards another time." We all rise, scatter around the room, picking up extra trimmings from the floor and placing the lose items back onto the front table. Gina flips the light switch and pushes the door open.

"You can all take your boards with you and hang them up in your cells," she states. Wow, what a prize, Gina. We all stamper out of the doorway one by one, eager like a flock of giraffes on a safari.

Chapter 16

The sun is beaming down through the trees, onto the courtyard. A cool breeze flows through. I close my eyes and absorb the fresh air. The leaves rustle in the wind, and helicopter seeds float down to the ground as I sit alone again with my notebook.

I am still trying to wrap my head around the proof of murder that Jared presented to me. If I continue to plead innocent, I face twenty-five years in prison. If I sign an agreement, I get ten years of prison time. Ten whole years is still a lot to me. That's my whole young adulthood. My life would lose ten years that I could be traveling and ten years that I could be attending college and then writing about my life. I can study anything in college. Maybe I can take creative writing classes, or theater, or maybe I can become a teacher or a guidance counselor.

I want to break out of here somehow. The thought has been running through my mind since Jared and I had that talk. I wish Jared would realize what he is doing. I wish he would acknowledge the fact that he does not want to be an attorney. Anyway, I jot down the word **ESCAPE** in bold capital letters, and then I doodle a stick figure picture of myself pulling two bars of my cell apart just enough to walk right through them. *I continue with my story Monster World.* It is the only thing keeping me sane right now.

James walks over to me and starts a conversation.

"How are you feeling today?" he asks.

I close my journal. The place where I have been writing all

my thoughts and plans and plotting ways of getting out of here.

"I'm feeling fine," I say. Then I peek over at a food van delivering boxes to the jail, and I start to wonder…

I lie in my bed with racing thoughts. I'm peeping pages of a Cosmopolitan magazine that Marci gave me. I'm not sure how she can focus enough to read these in here, but she does. As I turn the pages, I land on an article named, *how to know your crush is really into you.* I read two paragraphs before I declare it lame, and then I turn the page again to an article about a girl who developed a drinking problem after being sexually abused. I was more intrigued by this article because it is nice to read about stories like that in a beauty magazine.

The girl had been sexually abused by her stepfather. Her mom and her stepdad loved dogs. They had a black lab. Since her mom had to work so much, and her stepdad grew and sold marijuana, he was the one home all the time. She spent a lot of time at home with her stepdad, while her mom was busy managing the art gallery she owned. She worked late, and her stepdad would force sexual favors from the girl when she was a child. The dog was the only member of the family that seemed to have any respect in the household, so one day the girl decided to use her mom's painting supplies and paint a picture of the dog being blown up into many pieces. The dog's head, limbs, body, and tail were all in separate pieces next to a dark hole that represented where the bomb was set.

She hid the painting under her bed when she was finished, but one day she refused to do anything sexual with her stepdad, so he got angry and reached for his belt lying on the floor next to the bed. He was seemingly about to whip her with it until he saw the edge of the painting and pulled it out from under the bed. He was outraged by the painting, and he threatened the child that if she did not give him a hand job, he would show the painting to her mother. She did not want her mother to see her anger toward the dog, and she did not want anyone in the community to find out she wanted to kill animals, so she did what her stepdad asked.

Soon, her mother caught onto the fear the child had shown toward the stepdad, so she kicked him out of the home. Soon after, he got a court order, and then she admitted everything he did to the police, but they still forced her to go with the stepdad. The mother didn't know who the biological father of the child was, and since he had been a part of the child's life since she was two, he was able to define himself as a de facto parent.

Her life got much worse after the tragedy. She barely saw her mother until she didn't see her at all. She was raped many times and never called the police. She drank so much that her liver grew, and her doctor begged her to attend sobriety meetings and groups. So, she did, and she felt safe there, admitting that she had been sexually abused. She also made friends who also experienced these acts of cruelty. Then, she wrote a book, she started painting again, and she became one of the editors of Cosmopolitan. She found her mother and reunited with her. Her mother also developed a drinking problem, so the amazing woman brought her mother to her support groups. The two of them started juicing fruit together and started a mother-daughter business juicing fruit, just the two of them. Her mom also became a handbag designer and started her own TED talk about noticing the behavioral patterns of abused children.

What a beautiful story. It sent a shiver of euphoria up my spine. I really wish the daughter and the mother were together the whole time, instead of the nasty, selfish step-piece-of-crap.

I toss the magazine over the edge and slap my hands on the

mattress. I wish Mr. Cat-a-corn were here during this stressful time. I miss his little cat ears and googly eyes and sparkling unicorn horn.

I snap out of my imaginative moment thinking of the good old days with Mr. Cat-a-corn. I reach over to my notebook that I have placed between the mattress and the wooden bunk frame. I start writing a little more in *Monster World*. I write about how my robot teacher-nanny was not programmed to answer intuitive questions and how I found it odd that tiny drips of water dropping between my eyes was so torturous. It didn't matter to me.

I decide to strategize a plan to escape my robot nanny. My mom clearly doesn't care enough about me to take care of me herself. It is clearly so important to her to galivant around in her man suit? She must delegate her parenting duties to this piece of metal and hardwire machinery! This lousy piece of scrap is also rather alert. She "sleeps" like any computer sleeps for twelve minutes each day, but she locks everything up pretty good.

There's no way out of homeschool without waking nanny-robot. There's no way to kill nanny-robot either. So, as I sit here writing down my plans – so far, I have zero – my eyes wander into my closet, and a sweater had fallen off of its hanger dead in the center. As I make my way over to pick it up, draped over my Nike sneakers, the Nike Zoom sneakers, the ones you can only get directly from the factory, I reach for the sweater. I notice there is a bolted-up passageway right in my closet. It seems to be square-shaped and painted over with off white paint, revealing a difference in shade against the white wall. There are blocks of wood screwed into the passageway at all angles. I remember that my mom keeps a pink screwdriver in a secret compartment in her underwear drawer.

When I enter her room, I dare to pull the drawer open. Some condom wrappers, a TV guide, and a half-eaten bag of mini-Twix candy bars are here to greet me. I push them aside and pull open the flap that leads to the screwdriver. Once I have the appliance in hand, I rush over to my closet, and I start removing the screwed in wood to the passageway. Even after I accomplished that, the tiny door was still closed pretty tight, but I knew where to pull from because I could see the outline where the white wall turns to an off white. First, I use a painting knife to fit my way underneath the edge of the door, then once I've wedged it partially open, I continue to pull. Robot-nanny has four more minutes of sleep, so I must be quick. Just a few tugs and the door open wide, almost throwing me across the room.

I crawl back over to the tiny space with a flashlight. It's dark in there, but I can see a stairway and brick side walls of the narrow passage. I force myself to make my way down the stairs, hoping there's a window where I can escape, otherwise I need to get back before Robot-nanny wakes up from her nap! As I follow the stairway down to the bottom, I am greeted by someone dressed in all black with a hood carrying a lantern. He points his finger and directs me right to a window opening.

I thank the individual and I move a metal chair to sit directly under the window and I crawl right out into the sunshine. Dandelions are everywhere! I twirl around in the outside world...

Then I draw a blank again. I can't get my creative juices flowing in here! I shove my notebook back in its place.

"I need to get out of here, Marci. I need to escape."

"Chica, we all need to get out of this place."

"No, there's things I haven't told you," I say as soft as a

whisper.

I hear her moving around sitting up on her bunk.

"Girl, you know you can talk to me. Come down. Let's talk."

I climb down onto her bunk and begin my story.

"My attorney was my boyfriend before I came here." She gives me the hardest stare I've ever seen. I take a deep breath and rub my eyes. "We were supposed to go to L.A. to bring his story about zombies that turn into raccoons and make a movie."

Marci blinks fast in disbelief. She puts her clammy hand on my forehead.

"Girl, are you feeling okay? I mean, I believe what you are saying, but if you go around talking like this, you're going to be committed." She slaps her hand on my shoulder. I can tell she really doesn't believe me, but it's nice of her to play along.

"Well, I kinda already told my attorney. My court hearing is next Wednesday."

She removes her hand from my shoulder and slaps it against her forehead.

"What am I going to do with you?"

"I really need to escape, Marci. My hearing is next week! I'm thinking my way out could be the food van that comes by while we are out in the courtyard. How often is it there?"

"Once a week, alternating between Tuesday and Thursdays. So, next week it will be here the day before your court hearing. How convenient?" She lets out a sigh.

"Okay Leenah, I will help you in any way that I can."

She straightens and stiffens her back, and I give her a huge hug.

"I think me and the girls can distract the guard while you sneak into the van. Typically, the driver only brings a few boxes in for the week, but he must walk to the end of the south-end hall with them. I think I already have something in mind to distract the guard on duty."

"Ohhh... thank you, thank you, thank you!" I exclaim, giving her another hug.

"Anything for you, Leenah. One of my foster moms always told me that there is nothing more powerful than a woman who has nothing left to lose. I think we got this, chica. But where are you going to go?"

"I'll figure that out when I'm out of here."

Marci's eyes glisten as if she is trying to remain neutral when she really wants to cry. *Is she going to miss me?* I think so. I know I'm going to miss her.

"Okay, I trust you," she says as she gives me a hug that almost lifts my butt off the bed.

Marci is so kind to me, even though deep down she is hardcore. I wish we were related. Outside of jail I literally have no one, and in this cell, I feel like I never have to do anything on my own.

Jared made me feel like that on the outside, but he's a different person now. Apparently, we are in a different world now.

Marci and I burst into tears and cry on each other. A guard walks by and shakes her head. When we've wiped the last of our wet tears, and our cheeks have the remains, leaving them glazed with a sticky tight feeling, I head back up to my bunk and stare placidly at the ceiling. I imagine the times Jared and I star-gazed on the roof of The Cake House. Then, I really had to go pee. I slide my sheets down, jump off my bunk, slapping a marker on a metal bar, signaling a guard's attention, but not before I do the bathroom dance in the dark.

"I really have to pee," I tell Simone, and she lets me out. I meet Jolene in the bathroom as she's washing her hands.

"Jolene, I just have to ask you something," I say as I release the digested grape juice and six glasses of water I had before my chat with Marci. I finish locking the stall door in mid-piss. It seems like she paused to think about talking it up in the bathroom before bedtime, but she answers.

"Sure, what is it, Leenah?"

"Why are you here?" I finish and flush the toilet. When I exit, she's just standing there for a moment, staring at herself in the mirror. She doesn't even glance at me as I turn the faucet to wash my hands, but my eyes remain on her. "I mean, by the looks of your vision board I've gathered that you really have a lot going on outside of here. It definitely seems like your daughter needs you more than ever right now."

She breathes out hard through her nostrils. She hovers over the sink, head facing down and hands flat on the granite. "I started my own business designing children's bikinis."

I wait to process. First, I say the sentence over in my head that Jolene is in jail because she started her own business designing children's bikinis. "Wai... Wait a second... you are here because you started your own business designing children's bikinis?" The depth of my stare at her could swallow my eyeballs.

"My daughter was a swimmer, and it inspired me to get a job at the speedo factory. Then I got even more ideas." Her head sinks down lower.

"*Ugh*, does the government know where your daughter is right now because your vision board the other day does not make it look like she's out swimming in her mom's designer clothing?" I protest in disbelief, digging for more information.

"There's more..." she continues, holding back.

"Jolene, what is it? You can trust me…" She glares back up into the mirror.

"I started stealing the materials from the factory and designing my own children's bikinis. First for my daughter, but then her friends really liked them, and the other parents started complimenting. So, I started selling my designs, continuing to steal from my work." She sighs. "Next thing I knew, I was selling the bikinis on Etsy. I got away with it for a while until I started selling them at the farmer's market. That's when people started to report me. When the court hearings started, my ex filed for custody of my daughter, and since I could not afford to pay for the material, they agreed that I should do the time." The waterworks begin, and Jolene shifts her look directly at me. "He's a heroin addict, and everything that I pictured in that vision board is true. She doesn't want to be there; she doesn't deserve to have to be there. She wanted to be on the *Baby-Sitter's Club* show on television." She places both of her hands on my shoulders staring directly into my soul. "While I am in here, I've been knitting her a scarf from yarn I received from commissary, and I've also been writing her part in the *Baby-Sitter's Club* so she could be the new member. And sometimes, I don't think I am writing it fast enough because I am still here, and she is still there and…"

I reach my arms out, pulling her into a hug. I feel her sobbing into the shoulder of my jumpsuit. "Jolene, you are a really good mom. I cannot believe they did this to you. Your work should have understood."

"She would visit me in here, but only a few times before I could not take seeing her like this any more. Child welfare did nothing to help her, and from inside here, I begged. I used my one phone call a week to call them and have her taken away. The first thing she said to me the first time she visited was that she was hungry, and she was not allowed to eat until she finished her homework. She always had trouble with homework, but she had to complete it in order to eat anything at all." She starts to shake and pace back and forth, holding her face in her hands. "Her child attorney was only after money, his name was Miguel Fraznee, he looks just like Freddie Krueger!"

"Oh my God, Jolene! That is terrible! I cannot believe the government would allow such treatment. Ya know what..." I think about the conversation Marci and I just had about my escape, but I don't want to leave Jolene feeling like this either. "I am writing a story also. Let's make a secret meeting spot where we can share our stories with each other. You can share the one about your daughter, and I will share mine with you. It might help both of us heal."

She dries her tears and the snot running from her nose with her sleeve and shakes her head up and down. "Yeah, I would like that."

I really wish there was something I could do for Jolene. Here I am plotting my own escape, and there are women in here who shouldn't be here either. When we part ways, I have a hard time sleeping with Jolene's daughter on my mind. Also, I did not know there was yarn in commissary.

The guards slide crow bars up against the cells to wake us up. At breakfast time, I have a cheesy omelet, home fries, strawberries, and a chocolate chip muffin. It's delicious and complimented by coffee and orange juice. The girls are quiet, Marci has crusties in her eyes, and I feel the urge to start a conversation, but I'm reluctant.

The doctor I met in the hallway greets me as he stands at the end of the table.

"Well, hello there, Elise! Remember me? I would like to speak with you for a few minutes, and it looks like now would be a perfect time!" I glance down at my breakfast plate. "Oh, don't worry you can take your tray with you." I wave to the ladies, and I rise from my seat, following Dr. Davis to his office. His office is small, with a few pictures of the New England Patriots on the wall and a globe sits by the computer screen on his desk. It is the most culturally adapted room I have seen in this building. I'm invited to sit in a prestigious leather chair that matches the one he rests down in, and it's delightful. I may enjoy these spontaneous meetings after all.

"How are you feeling this morning, Elise? Did you sleep well? What number would you rate your mood between the numbers 1 and 10, 1 being absolutely awful and 10 meaning wonderful?"

"Let me think for a moment." I press my fork into the omelet on the tray I have placed on my lap, then I add a few home fries before shoving it into my mouth. I take a moment to recline in my chair as I chew, then I swivel from side to side, taking advantage of the luxury. "I would say I am a seven. I guess I slept okay, not as well as I hoped. I am having some nightmares about weird creatures coming back to haunt me. I no longer have fun-filled dreams of adventures with my long-lost mother." I take another bite of my breakfast. This is like being at a shrink's office in the movies. It feels great!

"Do you think your bad dreams are anxiety related?" *Sure, why not.*

"Yes, I am having a lot of anxiety here. My heart feels like it is banging like a drum on a daily basis!"

"Okay, well I am going to prescribe you some Trazadone for

the anxiety and sleep problems, Seroquel to regulate your mood, and are you feeling depressed at all?"

"Yes, I am sad."

"All right, well I will prescribe you some escitalopram for your depression."

"I am going to give you these written prescriptions, and I would like you to bring them to the nurse, and she will make note of the time in the evening I have written down for you to take the medicine." He smiles and hands me the papers. "Oh yes, and the nurse will need to do some bloodwork before you start taking the escitalopram, and during the duration you are taking the medicine."

Bloodwork? Fuck! He didn't say anything about bloodwork in the beginning!

He rises from his chair and opens the door. "I hope you have a nice rest of your day." I pull myself off the leather seat.

"Wait a minute, did I say depressed? Ya know, I wouldn't say that I'm really depressed, it's more like I feel a regular amount of sadness at times, only when appropriate."

"*Haha*, I will check back in with you in a few weeks, I am sure the medicine will work just fine." He proceeds to escort me out of his office giving a subtle push to my back and closes the door when I'm out.

Great, there's no way out of this bloodwork. I hate needles!

Upon my return to my cell after picking up my medicines and passing out in the nurse's chair for a few minutes after giving blood, I make a small note in my composition book about making the nurse a vampire in *Monster World*. Then, I feel compelled to plan the next move for my character in *Monster World*. All I can think about is that when she finally finds her way… into the woods, of course, there is a tiny old woman who could be a witch. She is holding Jared captive! But wait a second, should I still call him Jared in the story, because he looks like he could also pass as an Adam or a Lance. Anyway, the witch lures me into her cabin. It's great at first because she makes delicious food, and Jared and I get to spend time together, but there is something wrong with Jared. *He has puppet strings?* ... No. *He can't talk?* ... Maybe. *He has buttons for eyes?* ... Too cliche. I guess it isn't as easy as I thought to find something that could be wrong with Jared. My head hurts anyway, I'm sure something will pop into my mind soon enough.

Then a new guard, a petite blonde girl with the name Peatman printed on her uniform arrives, tapping her nails on the metal to get my attention.

"Your paperwork has been processed, Elise. We have the government notification of commissary for your stay here," she says, smiling and waving the paper on my side of the cell. "Do you need me to explain anything?" I hop down and grab the paperwork. I can't believe it; they are really going to pay me to stay in jail.

"No, I can read it just fine," I respond. Almost a thousand dollars a month, that's a generous commissary. I re-read the letter a few times, making sure I didn't miss anything before I scrunch it between my mattress and frame.

I'm consumed with boredom until Marci gets back in our cell after her encounter in the visitation room. She doesn't talk much about the people who visit her, but when she comes back to the cell, she usually has an energetic glow about her.

"Wanna play a game of UNO?" she asks, "or we can play monopoly. That's all I have for games, but I also have some nail polish if you want to paint each other's nails and play two truths and a lie." I opt to play the truth and lying game with nail painting, especially because when she opened her box of polish, vibrant colors with glittery tints caught my eye. I crawl down the latter onto the floor and we both sit Indian style. I pick out a light blue color labeled 'ripple reflect' and a gold color labeled 'high maintenance'. I figured she can paint my nails the blue color with the gold color on each ring fingernail. It looks glamorous the way I imagined it in my head.

"We can talk more about Jared and your escape plan if you want, Chica, we don't need to play two truths and a lie."

"To be honest, I'm so angry about the whole Jared thing. And look at this…" I refer back to my notebook, showing her the page where I wrote the whole heart-pouring letter confronting him about the importance of our relationship with each other. I rip it out of the notebook, crumple it up, and toss it into the trashcan.

"Also, Marci, I think I'm going to put a pin in escaping right away. I just got my commissary, and I'm interested in knitting."

"It's always the commissary that seems to keep people here." She laughs. "But suit yourself."

I spend countless hours after Marci and I paint each other's nails pacing back and forth in our cell. I'm filled with energy, too much energy to stay calm. It's hyperactivity again, I've felt it before at Claire's.

When the evening rolls around, I return to the nurse's office to swallow my cocktail of medicine and return to my mattress. Dr. Davis was right, the medicine put me right to sleep without constant temper tantrums from my heart ventricles and restlessness. Drifting into a deep, comfortable sleep is easy.

I meet Jolene in the commissary line. It's the first time I've been here. "What do we do?" I ask her.

"They call us into a small corner to pick out some items that we would like to use. You show them your letter, and they will hand you some coins to use for the day. There are some snacks, some healthy and some candy and cookies. There's also soda!" she exclaims.

"Yeah, Marci always gets soda. She shares a lot of her stuff with me."

"You can also pick out different color flip flops for the shower. In the beginning we all get those boring black ones, but at least they care enough to give us those ones at all." She shrugs.

"Anyway, when and where do you think we should have story time? I was thinking after lunch when we have some free time, but not in the television room, for obvious reasons. I know that's where everyone flocks to so we can just pick from any of the other activity rooms."

"Sure, after lunch works for me." James calls Jolene into the room to buy stuff. I am already thinking about making myself a scarf. *Oh, but what size needle should I get? What size yarn should I get? What color yarn should I get?* While my head fills with questions, I'm called in for my turn. I hand my paper to Simone, and she tells me I can spend $50 today.

"There's price tags on everything in there." I'm wondering why I cannot choose the amount of money myself, but I'm assuming they just don't do that here.

When Marci comes back to our cell, I have a set of turquoise knitting needles and some thick baby green yarn. I've already begun casting on and shoved two butter cookies into my mouth before she walks in with her bag and grunts as she dives into her pillow.

"Look, Marci, I got a Chinese Jasmine plant! I'm going to

train it to grow up the cell bars. And these fairy lights I strung over my bunk, I feel like I am in Tinkerbell's treehouse."

"That's great," Marci replies as I hear her cracking open a coke. I just let nature takes its course and not even ask why she sounds hissy because I don't want anything to kill my vibe. Especially since I am sailing on a cool wave of lavender with this gel mask.

"I forgot that I really wanted tie dye and gel pens. Why can't we choose how much money we take out? Going to commissary twice a week with $50 is not going to add up to almost a thousand dollars a month." I say aloud to myself.

"They save money for you so that you can get an apartment when you get out of here. Some people get out early on good behavior because they want to see what type of apartment they end up in. Then they end up back in here because apparently it wasn't what they expected," she responds.

I lick the cookie crumbs from my fingers. "Interesting."

Chapter 17

It's pulled pork lunch day. Jolene and I are scheduled to have story time in the recreation room. Scanning the cafeteria has me noticing that some people like to wear florescent beads on their bracelets or in their hair. I guess it's the only color to be added when your uniform is so 'blah.' Over the borderline mundane. I scoff my sandwich down, but I pick at the mini salad, carefully mounting one lettuce at a time into my mouth. I freeze when I acknowledge that someone in the corner of the room is dressed differently than my cell mates. I immediately bury my face in my hands. "No… why… here?" I reluctantly lift my head back up and move my retina without tweaking my neck. JEANNIE. I don't feel like reading any more, Jeannie, I'm writing now.

I pick up my tray and rush for the waste basket. Eyes on Jeannie, I run into an extremely tall woman who towers over me with a look of vengeance and slaps the tray out of my hand. As the remains from my food land on a woman from the crack head table, I run quickly past the guards and out of the cafeteria faster than a jack rabbit on the fourth of July.

"What happened today at lunch?" Jolene asks as we both scramble through our writings.

"Nothing, I just didn't feel well, but the nurse gave me some apple juice that made me feel a little better."

"Nice, I brought pineapple wine that I fermented outside in the garden by the courtyard." She places a mason jar in the middle of the table. "There are paper cups over in this cabinet here." She grabs a stack of paper cups and I purse my lips to one side. I'm not even going to ask because I have a Jeannie stalking me who brings me rodents. *How the hell did Jeannie even get there? Where was her bottle?* Anyway...

"So, who wants to go first?" I ask. Jolene Pours me a cup of wine.

"I just started my story entering my daughter Magnolia into the *Baby-Sitter's Club*. I think you will like it, Leenah."

I took a sip of my wine, and I gestured with my face for her to begin.

My name is Magnolia Frazzlebeem. I am happy to be the new student here at Stoneybrook Middle School. Unfortunately, my mother and I had to make an abrupt move from my old house because even though my father is filthy rich, he decided to ruin our reputation by using the cheapest drug available, heroin.

I press my lips together and raise my brows, but I also move forward, elbows on the wooden table. I've read the Babysitter's Club books, and I've watched the television show. This story already starts off rather peculiarly. It doesn't fit well, but I'm intrigued, nonetheless.

My mom made homemade wine from the grapevines on their land, but he indulged in too much, leaving my mother with nothing but bills, and soon everything was slowly being taken away anyway. My mom didn't want that to happen to me. She was a swimsuit designer as well. Everyone would soon find out that her husband was doing heroin, and she just could not live with that embarrassment.

Anyway, as I stare into the mirror exposing only myself and the packed-up boxes in the background, I feel sorry for myself because I can't even get up in front of the classroom when I arrive at my new school because I can't talk. I can't speak at all. I can only write down short sentences telling people what I need. This is going to be tough, being the new girl and having to explain everything to new people when they can't hear me at all. I freeze up and gaze at my blonde hair and blue eyes, very rare for a Latina. Still, it's me. My mom and I are still in our third story apartment, and my real dad is out traveling the world as a photographer. That's what my mom tells me. I never met him, but supposedly he's busy, and he writes me letters... or my mom writes me letters with his false address printed on the envelope. Her last boyfriend was a heroin addict, and my mom was paying all the rent, so she kicked him to the curb.

We have to leave because my mom worked at the Speedo factory, and she just stole a ton of fabric for her business. She also stole and sold a bunch of heroin from her ex-boyfriend. We must leave ASAP. So, luckily my mom found a small log cabin in Stoneybrook, Connecticut. Jolene's eyes light up and her voice is endearing.

I don't know how my mom got a hold of enough drugs to sell and get away with it to the point where we now have our own house AND she will be having her own bikini business, but she did it. When we were with Glenn, we couldn't even buy an area rug or wall paint, or a toaster oven.

I'm really nervous. I already can see it now that the teacher, with his Dunkin Donuts coffee in hand, is going to ask me to stand up and introduce myself to the class. My mom says being in school will only be temporary until we get settled and she can homeschool me while running her business. I hope that's the truth because kids at my old school would be so mean. They used *to ask me questions that required long answers so that my hand would cramp up while trying to write my response down on paper.*

Well, when we arrived at Stoneybrook, and we were unpacking our boxes, a nice girl named Claudia who was dressed like a Teen Vogue model greeted me with some giant chocolate chip cookies. She was very nice, but it was a little weird that I couldn't talk to her.

"I brought you these cookies, my mom and I knew someone was going to be moving in because the 'For Sale' sign had just been brought down. With my half-eaten cookie in hand, crumbs stuck to my lips and some falling to the new hardwood flooring, I shift my neck in all directions, but I must have misplaced my notebook!

"NO!" I gasp.

"Really," she replies and then she continues...

Where is it? The Pink 'Weekend Forever' notebook my mother just got me with her drug money before we arrived. Claudia is staring at me with her mouth open as I maneuver through all the packaging searching for the place where I can put my words.

"Do you need me to come back another time?" she asks. She looks so sweet. I am really interested in her and her clothing. My mom walks in carrying a large area carpet all rolled up for the living room.

"You are going to love this rug I bought from Michael's craft store. I went a little crazy there, and this rug is so vintage and – Oh, I see you have a friend here." Her eyes dart back and forth between Claudia and me.

"I just came by to bring some cookies." She places the

ceramic plate on the kitchen island. "I will come back another time, it looks like you two are busy."

"Oh, you are the sweetest. Magnolia is just a little shy at first." She eyeballs me, asking if she's verbalizing the correct excuse. "She has laryngitis right now." I close my eyes and take in a large breath of air. "She will be better in no time, so we cannot wait to have you around again." My mom plops the rug on the floor and begins to unravel it as Claudia scurries out the door.

After sharing what I have already written in *Monster Land*, I'm feeling a buzz takeover. The wine that Jolene made was delicious and inexplicably strong. It made me crave our next story reading encounter. This time, Jolene brought homemade Angry Orchard hard cider, made with real crisp apples. I really don't know how she does it. It is time for me to start.

I gallop through the forest filled with the most beautiful wildflowers and rose vines growing like a fence between and up the oak and the maple. I Trollip through the Evergreen. Suddenly, I hear more crackles of leaves and twigs, more than what is carried by my own two feet! I come to a halt and listen. I can hear the birds singing and the leaves sweeping off of the trees and scraping against each other. Then I hear it again, there's another set of feet here, I don't move a muscle and for a moment I realize there may be more. My heart is like a butterfly ready to break out of my ribcage and leave this soon to be crime scene of my expected death.

The longer I remain in place, the louder the sound gets with proof that it is moving closer to me. If I move, the feet will come closer at a more rapid pace. I didn't make the track team in middle school. Strenuous exercise is not my thing. Light walks and a short sprint are, but that really doesn't matter right now.

The footsteps multiply as they grow near. My heart still thumping. At this point, why can't a meteorite just fall from the sky in my direction? Before I knew it, there was a person standing by each tree circling me. They had guns in hand, but all of them were down by their sides. It's silent for all of ten minutes. Then the older woman speaks.

"Nobody makes a threatening move! We want her to feel safe with us. What is your name, dear?"

"Olive," I respond.

"Olive, we would like you to come live in our village with us, North of here in Vermont." She sounded sweet, but I've known others before who sounded sweet. She had short, very dark hair and spoke with some sort of European accent that I wasn't sure of yet.

By the looks of things, it didn't seem like I had a choice. I motion in a circle and find that there's a mixed group of adults and children and the one old lady. The next thing I know I'm riding in a pickup truck with five cousins in the back. And that's when the title changes to... Vermontville-the Devil's Forest.

A week into the village in Vermont was a lovely experience, there were so many trees around, there was a large house and a barn, wooden Swing sets hanging from the tree, a nighttime fireplace, and something called a dingle. Which was really a pathway through the forest that brought you back to where you started. There were fireflies at night, and one lonely trip around the dingle showed me that there were fairies involved in this adventure. So, for a while I would walk around the dingle with my so-called cousins, but the fairies would only come out when I was alone. I would share some random stories about the weirdness in how the adults acted like they were the same age as the children, all taken care of by one older adult. They left me money every time. So, one night, Lauren – one of the cousins, my favorite one (she kind of looked like me and I trusted her) – wanted me to tell her a story so I started randomly talking about the fairies, but she noticed a lot. She paid very close attention that I was not expecting, and she said, "Hey, that is not a fictional story, you are talking about our village! You have been talking to fairies here!"

"No, no I haven't," I protest, standing up tall in her face.

"Yes, you have! You replaced the dingle with the woolly triangle."

She caught me, and there was no turning back because once Lauren knew something, she knew something. So, I told her to just go see for herself then.

"Go see for yourself then, I don't care." I slam down the wheat bushes and the yellow and purple flowers we picked in my basket down so hard that they scattered everywhere, and the breeze took the rest. She went to go see what I was talking about in my story. When she came back, I was coloring with Danielle and Mandy. She grabbed me by the arm and escorted me up the stairs to the highest level of the middle house.

"I saw something…" She was paler than usual and looked petrified.

"What did you see, some fairies… whoop dido you saw what you wanted." I shoot her an eye roll.

"No, I didn't see fairies. I saw dead children." I gasped.

"Dead children," I repeat.

"Not just any dead children, Olive, I saw a dead Mandy and a dead Holly and a dead—"

I cut her off as she was about to continue naming dead

cousins. *"You are telling me that you saw our cousins lying down in the forest dead?"*

"Worse, they were walking dead."

Jolene finishes off a whole cup of wine in three large gulps and pours herself some more. She sips off the top and moves her body closer, her chin rested in her palm. She slides in even closer.

"What do you mean walking dead?" I yelp. She closes the door. "Be silent, Grandma Maryanne cannot find out about this, she will probably like die or something." I BEGIN TO PROCESS THE ENTIRETY OF WHAT SHE HAS EXPLAINED.

"Lauren, how do you know you are even aloud to tell me this?"

"I-I didn't really think about it, I just assumed because me and you are the only children, I didn't see dead versions of."

"Did they say anything to you?" She takes a gulp so loud it could wake a bear during hibernation.

"Mandy with the ax in her head warned me to warn you about talking to the fairies." She cringes, followed by a soft sputter leaving her lips, chest rising with an inhale.

"Annnd... the consequence if I continue...?"

"Well, I don't know that part, but—"

"Oh, God Lauren, not another assumption..." I palm my forehead.

"Well, this is the part that I'm assuming that since we are the only children, I haven't seen dead, I will start seeing us... ya know... dead." I ponder for a moment. I don't want to stop talking to the fairies. I'm saving up the money that they give me so I can buy my own land one day.

"Okay, well I guess we can just go around the dingle

together then. Maybe we won't see anyone, or maybe we will see both, but I suppose we shouldn't tell the others about this especially the... adults? God damn it, Lauren, why aren't the adults adults?"

She shrugs. It's Grandma Maryanne's way."

"Or else what?" After the look on her face I respond, "Never mind, I already know what you are going to say."

*

It's meatloaf dinner night, and I can't help but notice that Marci is still acting a little odd toward me. She's barely talking, and it's conjuring up an eerie vibe in the whole table. I'm saved by the bell when Dr. Davis calls me into his office again. Something is eating away at her, I know it. It's giving me a headache.

When Dr. Davis has me behind his closed door, he announces in private that he needs to check my head for lice.

"My head isn't itchy though," I say right before there's a tickle behind my ear.

"It's precautionary. Someone may have entered here with a bit of an infestation problem," he replies.

The next thing I know, I'm hairless in a large room with half of A pod, B pod, and a minority of C pod. We all decided to shave our heads after realizing the shampoo solution was only a temporary fix. There's a whole another room filled with a mix of infested cell mates. Our mealtimes were rearranged accordingly and everything. Gina decided to host a knitting class during Jolene and my story time, so we decided to move it to midnight. Marci was in our room, and there was a greenhouse area built off of our section where some girls chose to hang out. Well, Marci still wasn't speaking to us for a little while, until she decided to interrupt the beginning of our next story time with a discovery. She had a Ouija Board.

"It was on clearance in commissary," she says. Well, Marci didn't exactly know what we were doing during our secret story time, but she brought up another idea for a midnight activity.

"Ouija board?" Jolene swallows the lump in her throat.

"What's the harm, right?" I slide my notebook off to the side, and I notice Jolene does the same so she must agree.

"One of my foster brothers Madeia, told me that the Ouija board is the best way to contact your ancestors. I figured we could do that here," Marci says. "I found out that my great abuela, Esparanza Lopez invented the Quinceanera after she lost her virginity on her sixteenth birthday, and a thousand white doves sprinkled glitter and Mardi grass beads all over the land." Marci looks up through the window ceiling with both hands caressing her chest, and I follow her gaze into the dark speckled sky. When I check on Jolene, she looks puzzled, and I shrug.

And my great titi made the best homemade Puerto Rican salsa that she gave out to the immigrants arriving to America right off the boat. Something they don't tell you in history class because they're too busy talking about issues with every other race. Anyway, I found that out at my own Quinceanera. According to the rules, you find ancestors that have been in your position. So, we could literally find out if any of our ancestors have been incarcerated."

"That sounds like it would be interesting." I'm concerned about Jolene because I don't think she finds the idea quite as intriguing, but she nods.

"Okay, so let's start now," Marci implies as she has already taken the board and planchette out of the box. "No need for directions, I already know how to play." She tosses a folded-up piece of paper that slid out with the board over her shoulder.

"We each place all our fingers excluding our thumb onto the planchette in the middle of the board. We ask the board a question, and it spells out the answer... simple."

Chapter 18

*After some thought, my mom decided to surprise me and tell me that she was going to homeschool me after all for now and that I could learn a lot from her business. She also explained that she had talked to Claudine's parents and that I can start being social in her little "gatherings" before I step right into Stoneybrook Middle School. I guess this was a bit of a relief. Maybe if I can talk in a safe space, I can talk in front of a class full of my peers. I sigh, and that is **if** I talk.*

A gathering? I bet it's some secret society where they do witchcraft and sew clothing from the veins of their enemies! Just one meeting with Claudia and I already know she's unique like me! She was wearing Fox print farmer jeans and a sparkly knitted pink sweater with amethyst beads and tassel earrings! Oh yes, she does witchcraft! My mom is good at scoping them out too, since she's a designer.

I dig through my closet that night to find something suitable for the first time I meet the ladies. Mom was up watching a show called, 'Manifest', and I thought to myself how I really need to start spending some quality time with her. She looks so lonely.

"Mom, I found some fabric that I really like, but I would also like to cut it up and make a mess all over this shirt." I show her a plain white shirt that exposes one of my shoulders.

"It just needs a little bit of color!" We both say at the same time. Her look of excitement fills the room with memorable delight. As a mother daughter craft time, we make something a

little too extreme, and I decide to save it for just the right occasion. I spend the rest of my night anticipating my meeting with the girls and coming up with new projects to surprise my new friends.

They babysit? Boy did I misjudge Claudia and her gang. How could my mom use the word "gathering" so lightly? False advertising at its finest. Claudia guides me into her room filled with ice cream pillows, toucans, cheetahs, fabric paint and GEL CRAYONS! I want them.

"This is Magnolia," Claudia says chipperly. "She's my new neighbor." They're all staring at my rabbit mask. I made it and decorated it with gemstones and feathers. I made them masks too; I figured it would be a good uniform for when we trail off into the cemetery and dig up the bodies of those whose tombstones portray the biggest investment. I guess that won't be happening after all since a babysitting business won't have time for that.

I scan the room to meet the eyes of the club. "Magnolia, this is Mary Anne, our club president." Mary Anne waves. "I like your mask. I've been asking my mom and new dad for a pet rabbit. Do you have any babysitting experience?" she asks. She makes me a little nervous, and I open my notebook to jot down some words. I must tell them I can't babysit because nobody can hear me.

"Um, guys, I noticed on the walk over here that Magnolia does not speak, she writes everything down in her notebook."

"Does she know how to speak?" I hear the dark-skinned one with long black braids ask Claudia.

"Well, I'm not really sure." She turns to me. I appreciate Claudia speaking for me as it is my first time entering the room, *and she seems to know what to say to the group. I can't count on Claudia to say everything for me. My mom got into the habit of doing that, and I still don't talk to anyone.*

I write down with my ball point pen that writes shiny, smooth black printed words onto the note pages.

Sorry, I do not babysit.

"That's okay, you can still hang out with us. Look how creative she is. She made all these masks for us. These are actually great for the children. She may have some other good ideas up her sleeve. Mimi once told me that when you have lost one of your senses, your others become amplified. Which means that she can still contribute to our business without having actual contact with the children." Claudia is super smart and nice. She gets me, I can tell. I am relieved from my previous state of anxiety as I make my way into the circle of friends and sit down on the plush carpet.

I cannot believe my eyes! "Marci, what is it?" She has her flashlight on something crouched down beside the tree stump. We are forbidden out here, and there are no guards in sight, but they forgot to set the alarm on the greenhouse. We wandered a little too far. Marci moves forward, and Jolene and I are holding each other behind her, but when she shines her light directly on the being, he turns around holding his chest, both hands covered in blood. Jared? He's still breathing; we must do something. Well, he's actually panting, and his face is in shock. He looks toward me. Marci drops her flashlight. She's shaking, and she can't move.

"Marci? We need to do something."

I turn to Jolene. "Jolene, we must do something." It is like I am debilitated from screaming out loud until we all can do it in unison. I've seen Jared dead before. This sounds really bad and stereotypical, but I assume Jolene and Marci have seen something like this before also. We should all know what to do.

"He's going to die!" I yelp. "We should just go back now."

"You're not going anywhere," Marci whispers. "Something has already punctured his ventricle artery, he's going to die in a matter of minutes anyway," she states.

"He's going to die! We must do something!" I pull away from the group, but Jolene catches my arm.

"If anyone finds out that we were out here, we will be the ones accused of this murder. Elise, you already have a murder charge pending. Do you really want this?"

Jolene was right. Plus, the door to the greenhouse was unlocked. We will never be able to sneak out again. Oh no! my aching heart is throbbing. My poor Jared. He has been through so much! I keep seeing him expire! We all head back to the greenhouse together when Jared collapsed to the ground. I held the door while Jolene and Marci found two shovels. All I could think about was the fact that I now have seen three dead bodies, and Jared's twice.

That night, Jared came into my dream. He came to my cell and opened it up. Even as I stood in the doorway, he pushed himself in and we made out all the way over to my bunk. I took his clothes off as he removed my jumpsuit, kissing my neck. He sat down on my bunk, pulling me on top of him and pushing himself inside of me as he massaged my nipples. It was amazing, but when I woke up, the pound in my chest was still there because Jolene, Marci, and I had buried him right before that. I couldn't keep this inside of me any more.

"So, you're saying Jared died... and then... he died again." Dr. Davis was writing it down in his notebook with a perplexed look on his face, and I couldn't believe that I had just told him. Before all of this started, the Warden, Pauline Howard, had walked in on Jolene and I reading our stories out loud. Jolene became depressed when she ripped her story up because *The Babysitter's Club* already has an author. She threw it right into a barrel, lit a match, and burned Jolene's hard work. She told us that it is plagiarism, and she will not allow it in her jail.

Prior to that, us three girls had been playing Ouija board and it led me to find a book in the library called, *Finlay Donovan Is Killing It,* which led me to believe that my mom was actually out there writing books because the author described a girl named Delia who seemed to have a personality like mine and a relationship with my mom that I could vaguely remember. Delia was into Barbies and was very messy. It also led Marci to gather us outside to dig something up underground which didn't end up happening because we saw Jared. The Ouija board said there would be a locket outside of the greenhouse. Of course, when we found that the greenhouse was unlocked, we were then left in front of a murder scene.

And of course, Dr. Davis thinks that I'm crazy and he upped the dosages on my meds. I'm here in his office, and I just told him everything. I had brought up the idea of breaking free to Jolene after her story was tossed, but she just put her head down and said, "I'll just finish my time." Now I know I need Marci's help and I need to get out of here. Luckily, Marci doesn't know that it was Jared, my attorney, who we killed... I mean... watched die.

Later that day I find myself staring at the ceiling again

feeling immense sympathy for Jolene. I still have my own story and Jared's story. Reaching my hand in the crack between my mattress and bedframe, I pull out the scraps of Jared's laughable story. My eyes are pulled into the next event to untangle.

My next stop is even more gratifying. My mom was pulled away from me when I was nine, but before that she used to take me to the Carson Center for children. There, I spent countless hours talking to my therapist about how my mom spends too much time on her computer and on random dating apps on her cell phone. My mom didn't know that I watched her swipe carelessly left and right for meaningless encounters with men.

This obviously disappointed my therapist, though she didn't display this type of attitude in the beginning. She handed me back off to my mother, and we went on our way to enjoy some ice cream or a candy and a soda. Soon, child welfare was involved, and my beloved mother was taken from me. I am going to march my way over to that center and defecate all over her client paperwork for doing this to me and my mother!

I stop there. There's a common theme in my life where I am reading about abuse or long-lost mothers, and it resonates. This is it. The last of what I am reading from Jared's story. I need to make my own story worth something. Jared is gone and I need to accept that. If I don't accept that my life will probably go on and on, and I will continue to see Jared alive and then dead again. I cannot do this to my heart any more! It throbs so intensely for my beloved Jared, but I can't keep hanging on to what might have been. Claire could be right about Jared even though this whole time I've been focusing on what Jared has been saying about Claire! There are just too many overwhelming emotions pumping through my body. I don't know what to form my own opinion out of.

Chapter 19

I've been trying to focus on my real prison escape plan. Marci says she has it covered, and I trust her. The day has finally come. Going outside for my last outdoor break brings me a favorable feeling.

Tiny black squirrels wrestle for an acorn and chase each other up to the drainage pipe near the building's roof. The trees are still hanging onto what is left of their colorful leaves. One tree placidly rests in the corner with its vines sprawled out in every direction, and its leaves are all yellow. It reminds me that we can grow and hold ourselves together wherever our roots settle. What would happen if someone were just to come by unexpectedly with an axe and chop this magnificent tree down? To the far right, there's another tree, all green with just a touch of orange. It takes longer for some trees to change, I suppose.

Other trees around me are losing their leaves more rapidly. It's strange how they are content with undressing in the colder seasons, the birds and other little creatures exposed upon their branches. I wonder what it feels like to be a trunk of branches and leaves outside of a lifeless prison.

The food truck should arrive soon. There's an unsettling feeling in my stomach, and my nerves are on edge. Marci didn't exactly tell me how she plans on distracting James, but she said I'll know when I see it. We play ping pong together to keep our cool. I'm really going to miss her. At least I can say that I finally met someone who truly supports me.

She slides me a wink halfway through our game, and she grabs ahold of the ball, raising it in the air. She motions toward a chubby Hispanic girl across the courtyard. The girl starts taking off her jumpsuit and runs around with the top of her jumpsuit down, revealing her D-cup breasts. Then everyone, including Marci, starts doing the same and sprinklers begin to go off, spraying water all over the yard. James is running around in circles trying to catch up with everyone, and to my left, I see the food van arrive. That white piece of metal with the words FRESH FOOD written on the side is my free ticket out of here!

I watch as the women are running around half naked under sprinklers, and James calls other guards for back up. The driver of the food van pauses for a moment before getting out. I start to sweat because more guards will be out here soon, and I don't have much time. Marci eyeballs be to get going. I give her a look of frustration due to desire to shut down and call the whole thing off. What do I need to break out of jail for anyway? They feed me, and I have a cool roommate.

Oh, God damnit Elise! You want to make more of your life. Even ten years behind bars is a significant amount of time. I would have to travel far from here. Heck I may have to journey to London or whatever. At least they speak English there. I can go write some bloody books and go to bloody school in London.

Marci looks unimpressed by me just standing here conceding to my inner monologue. The other girls look rather joyful running around, dodging guards like a game of catch me if you can. It's like it is the first time they've been happy and felt the gift of freedom in a while.

Finally, I see the driver get out, and he opens the back doors. He reaches in to grab a huge box. At first, he struggles with it, and I get scared, thinking he's going to ask for help, and there will be another person to dodge. He places it down for a moment and then grabs a steady hold of it. When I see him walk into the jail, I catch a side glance of guards entering the courtyard, so I run and hide behind a bush. Luckily, there are bushes lining this side of the building, so I creep my way over to the van.

I almost can't breathe as I'm chuckling at what Marci conjured up for a distraction. *How did she get the sprinklers? How did she get the participants to help us?* I suppose this is just another fun activity. I feel bad I can't take them with me.

My heart is beating as fast as a cheetah rushing through open grassland. My palms are sweaty. I'm like a dichotomy of both excited and nervous.

I manage to crawl into the van like a rabbit moving its way through a hole in the ground. I find a spot behind some boxes near the seats and realize I will have to fight and run when my hiding spot is removed. Marci is right, *where are you going to go?* When I find a spot between some boxes stacked up high and the passenger's seat, I spot another prisoner crouched down behind the driver's seat, already ripped open a box of food, and has her hands buried in a bag of trail mix. The driver stops to have a conversation with someone in the kitchen crew, probably about all the commotion going on outside.

"Denise? You have a peanut allergy. You can't be eating that." As I reach to grab the bag out of her hand, she slaps my hand and stuffs a handful of the trail mix into her mouth.

"Oh my God!" I cross my arms over my chest. "Did you lie about having a peanut allergy? How did you pull that off? I thought you needed proof?" She gives a wide stretched smile.

"Well, if you really need to know, I walked in on the nurse smoking herb in her office one day. *Haha*, she had a blow-dryer in one hand and a rolled joint in the other. She was like this…"

She holds up her hand pretending to smoke a joint and hold a blow-dryer in her other hand. "She forgot to lock her office door. I told her I wouldn't say anything if she puts it in writing that I have a peanut allergy. I'm friends with Greg from the kitchen, he snuck me some goodies that contain nuts."

"*Hahaha.*" I notice in the rearview mirror of the van that the food guy is coming. "Oh, *shhh, shhh*, he's coming." I hold my finger up to my lips, and I motion for us to lower our heads.

Looks like Denise and I are in the same boat right now. This is helpful actually, having an escape partner. Plus, she's a con artist. I catch my breath and steady my trembling hands. I still have little time to plan out what I'm going to do after this. Denise may already have a plan. Maybe I can go back to Claire's. Or… maybe not because I was arrested there. I guess I will have to run until I find a place to call home.

The man comes closer and closes both back doors. Closing us inside. My hands begin to tremble again. The commotion outside dies down, and that was probably the end of today's outdoor time for the ladies. The girls risked losing their outside breaks for me.

A tear drips down my cheek and I wipe it. I can hear the crunching of leaves as the driver moves to the front seat and opens the door. Oh crap, I started writing a brilliant story, and I left it between my mattress and bunk frame. I left Monster World in prison! I also left my letter for Jared crumpled up in the wastebasket. At least I didn't write his name on it.

"Hey! You forgot the fruit." A man yells from the building."

"Oh yeah, sorry about that."

The driver treads back to the back doors and opens them up. I'm anxious and praying that the box isn't close and can't reveal that Denise and I are in here. That would be another ten years of jail time added to my twenty-five.

I close my eyes as he grabs a box closer to the doors.

"Sorry again about that," he says. Then I watch him wave goodbye through the tiny window in the back door.

I'm crouched against the passenger seat. He comes around again and opens the front driver's side door. I hear the key turning and loud exhaust. We head down the driveway with my heart still racing. The rocks bouncing off the tires. Denise looks like she doesn't have a care in the world. She just hustled herself onto a free ride out of prison. I wonder what she did in the first place. I can just imagine her shoplifting expensive electronics trying to convince the owner she can't help it because she has 'kleptomania.' She continues to take bites of the soft raisins and peanuts in the trail mix, careful not to take a bite of anything crunchy.

I close my eyes, and I picture Jared with his lost dreams and the fact that I had no way to save him. I think of what a great friend Marci has been to me. She grew up in several different foster homes, with parents giving up on her, and there was still so much good in her.

We drive down the road for a while. The bearded fellow driving clicks the radio on to the song 'Rhiannon' by Fleetwood Mac. He begins to sing at a very high volume and let's just say he can't carry a note in a bucket. Denise and I give each other disgusted expressions. She opens her mouth and points her finger inside. I cover my ears because such a beautiful song is drowned out by the horrific, raspy voice of a clearly tone-deaf food truck driver. I try to stuff my head between my knees, silently praying for the radio to explode. When the song finally ends, a man interrupts the station with a brief announcement.

Denise mouths out the words, *oh, thank God.*

"If you are sick of your day job, and you believe you have the singing talent to become one of America's Favorite Singers, then you're in luck. We are holding auditions in Hartford, CT this Saturday!"

"Holy crap! I better write this information down!" The driver clicks on his signal and pulls over smoothly onto the side of the road.

Oh My God! I mouth to myself and Denise. This guy actually thinks that he has singing talent.

When I hear him shuffle through some papers on the passenger seat and the clicking sound of a pen, I know he means business. He quickly jots down the information from the guy on the radio station, and I hear the pen clicking sound again. He tosses the paper into the glove compartment.

"My mom will be so proud of me. She always said I had a lovely singing voice." Well, his mom was either deaf or she didn't know how to tell the truth. We pull back into the road, and I was relieved to hear the sound of commercials on every station he lands on after that. I shift my mind to the unavoidable escape plan I need to conjure up when this truck does come to a stop. When I searched through Marci's things, I found a switch blade she had somehow snuck into the cell and kept safely under her mattress. I thought about taking it, but then I figured she must have had a really good reason to keep it around. I had no weapons, no distractions. Plus, it isn't this guy's fault Denise I escaped from jail. If he does try to stop us from running when it is time for me to get out of the vehicle, I do have those tai Kwan doe lessons I took in middle school. I will inflict too much pain on the big guy, just enough to get passed him.

Suddenly, I hear tiny raindrops falling on the roof like the sky is weeping over us. I imagine the sound of windchimes on a stormy afternoon, singing songs as the storm blows through, with raindrops forming puddles in the background for aftermath play.

The sound of rain transforms into millions of sharp needles pouncing off the roof. It gets louder like angry slashers in a horror movie using their sharp knives to break inside. I peek a little between the passenger seat and the door.

To my astonishment I see a bruised storm cloud rolling in, and it's enormous. The cloud looks angry and vexed. We skid a little and a lightning bolt strikes the telephone pole on the right side. The poll starts to lean a bit, and the lightning bolt strikes again! This is no forgiving storm.

The poll tips over in front of us. Surely it has learned a lesson. We skid to a halt and then slide into the poll. The crash causes us to tumble down a hill and everything turns black.

I descend into the darkness and its gravitating pull. I see books, rabbits, bicycles, stars, and various types of cakes are ascending upward-opposite of me. I smell chocolate and sanitizer at the same time. Mr. Cat-a-corn flies by, but he's going up, and I can't reach him. There's no sign of Denise anywhere, or the food truck driver. The gravitation pulls harder at my body, as the hook of an umbrella catches the back of my shirt to lift me up. The gravity grows stronger, and the umbrella unlatches. I hit a mound of mud and pebbles. There is nothing but darkness around me and it's quiet. But then I look up. There seems to be signs of light twinkling like floating stars in the distance.

Chapter 20

I open my eyes to a bright light shining on blurry faces I can't make out. One face moves in closer and is barely recognizable.

"It's okay, dear… you're in the hospital."

When my eyes finally come to focus, a familiar face that brings me back to early childhood is brought to light. It's… my mom! She has cocoa brown hair like me and hazel eyes. I remember her from a dream where we are both chasing the cotton candy at the end of the sky near the ocean. In another dream we are rescuing sheep from a farm. My mom was so strong, she defeated the vicious wolf who demanded conformity. We gave those sheep makeovers after. Some of them wanted their wool colored. In one of my favorite dreams, we are floating on the moon catching ice cream in waffle cones under millions of stars shining in the dark sky. Nothing else compares to this one dream where I was searching for her lost in the rainforest, and when I finally found her, she was eating tropical fruit with a family of monkeys under a tree canopy.

Her voice is familiar too. It's cultured and medium pitched – very feminine and comforting. I look down at my hands that have needles injected into my veins, then I notice a fluid pouch on the right side of me.

"Wh-what happened?" I ask as I try to lift my head from the pillow, and I'm yanked back by a throbbing headache. Then I hear another familiar voice and a blurry face standing near my ankles.

"You were riding your horse, Bruno, and he took off into the woods where he got scared and lifted his front hooves, tossing you off. You hit your head pretty hard, and you've been in a coma for a month." As my eyes move into focus, I realize that I recognize this voice matched to a familiar face.

"Marci?" I ask.

"Yes, I'm your riding instructor." *My riding instructor is Marci?* I focus in on her. She looks so young and there's no visible scar on her cheek. She still has long hair that naturally hangs down – almost to her waistline. The tattoos are still planted on her arm. I squint to see a wedding band and a nicely sized diamond on her left-hand ring finger.

"Where's Denise?" I ask.

"Who is Denise, darling?" My mother's face is puzzled. I roll my eyes up to think for a moment and purse out my lips. My face feels numb.

The nurse walks in to bring me a cup of water. "Is there a Denise here in the hospital?" my mom asks him.

"I'm sorry, we cannot give out that information."

"Oh, okay. It's just that my daughter just asked us about a girl named Denise, and I thought that maybe someone had spoken to her while she was in her coma or something. There isn't a nurse or doctor named Denise?" she asks, seemingly desperate to meet my needs. When the nurse walks out my mother assures me that there is no one named Denise here.

"So, I wasn't… horseback riding with a girl named Denise?"

"No, sorry, honey, we don't know anyone named Denise. You were all by yourself when you fell off Bruno. Perhaps you were dreaming about it in your coma or something? You have other friends who are here to see you, but we will only let them in if you are ready. Would you like us to let them in?" my mom asks as she changes the subject and fluffs my pillow underneath me.

"Sure, I would love to see them." I'm still feeling whoosie but so curious as to who else could be here for me. My heart begins to thump like heavy hands beating against a drum. I'm also quite anxious to find out who these 'friends' could be since my mom rose from the dead and my Ludlow Jail sorority sister shows up as my riding instructor.

My mom lets two high school kids in the door, and they excitedly dash toward me full of smiles reaching from ear to ear. I'm in disbelief when I find that the two high school kids are Julianna and Jared! Now I'm really starting to wonder how young I am! It's as if we keep dying and engaging in time travel. Or maybe the travel machine is broken, but we keep putting quarters in to make it work.

Jared digs into his backpack and pulls out a piece of paper.

"I know this is so sudden after you have been in a coma and all, but I can't wait to show it to you!" He holds the piece of paper up high in his hand. "You were the one who told me all of this would work out! So, here it is! Here's the flier for the play I wrote, and I will be directing. Tryouts are next week." He hands me the flier, his cheeks blushing to a cherry red. I stare down at the Bold headline. **Zombies in the Street**.

"Oh my God, Jared! Of course, I want to be a part of your play." This is wonderful. Jared is in this time zone doing what he loves – and his eyes light up again to confirm my theory.

"Do the zombies turn into raccoons?" I gaze up at him with a delightful grin.

"They don't, but that's a really clever idea for the next play," he says. We all chuckle.

The nurse comes in again and tells everyone that I am going

to need more rest. The whole gang says "Okay" simultaneously, and they begin to depart from the room. My mom stops and gives me some extra kisses.

"Um, where's my dad?" I blurt out before she walks away. She stops in mid-movement, her back facing toward me. She places her hand on her forehead and turns back around facing me.

"I had a feeling you would ask that," she says, glancing down for a moment, seemingly gathering up the right words to say at this time. "He passed away when you were three years old."

"Oh," I say, unsure of whether my mom had experienced any abuse. I guess this conversation can be continued later.

Julianna runs back to me.

"You had me so worried," she says, throwing her arms around me, giving a tight squeeze. I welcome her embrace because I am so happy to see her again.

"Julianna, how old are we?"

"We are fifteen – sophomores in high school. Well, Jared is sixteen."

I cannot believe it. We are all younger now... but I have people I care about, and I'm not going on trial for murder. My mom is alive, and I have the chance to get to know her again and build a better life for myself. Jared is doing what he loves, and evidently, he is one of my best friends. This is the type of not making sense I would never trade.

On the way home, my mom tells me that I am an honor student and that she thinks Jared has a crush on me. I can feel the blood rush to my cheeks. Thinking about the fact that Jared and I spend time together, it has become apparent to my mom that he likes me!

I wonder how my mom is taking care of me by herself, but then she tells me that she receives a lot of help from Marci and the employees at The Cake House.

When she mentions The Cake House, I freeze.

"You work at The Cake House?" I ask in a cautious tone.

"I own The Cake House," she says delightfully.

We drive by the bakery, and she points it out. It looks the same, with the delectable treats in the window. Perhaps it looks too much the same. When I look at the cake and the sign, all I can think of is that repugnant, red-headed swine. The street that surrounds the place is too familiar as well. Claire absolutely adored the Cake House. Now my mom does just as much.

We arrive at a cottage with a cement driveway and a fresh lawn filled with crows. The house is blue with red shutters and has a tiny deck filled with wind chimes. As we pull in closer to the garage, the flock of crows planted on the lawn fly into the partly cloudy sky. I scurry out of my mom's outlander and squabble up the steps to the front porch, flourished with hanging spider plants and lined with flowerpots. I turn the knob to the ivory door with anticipation. I creep in the doorway; the walls are vibrant light blue. The living room looks cozy with a casual theme and a medium sized television set. The kitchen has dark blue cabinets, modern-style appliances, and wallpaper with sketches of flowers uncolored. I reach into the cabinet to pull out a glass, grab a handful of ice from the freezer, and pour myself a refreshing glass of water.

I make my way to a large mirror in the hallway before heading to investigate the rest of the home. I'm about an inch shorter than I was before – my hair barely reaching my shoulders. I inch my way further down the hallway and reach a door with a wooden sign and the words Elise's Room carved into it. I open the door. My room is spring green with a My Hero Academia anime comforter. There's artwork decorating my walls, and there are fairy lights all over. Mr. Cat-a-corn is sitting upright against my pillow. I think I'm going to like it here. In this place in time.

"Elise!" Julianna scurries into my room. She surveys the area from the doorway with her body resting against the frame.

"Your mom clearly had some time to tidy up your room while you were in the hospital." She takes a deep breath through her nose, inhaling the vanilla lavender scent of Febreze still lingering in the air. "No offense, but your room is always trashed, with dirty clothes thrown into a big pile in front of your closet and draped over your bed and vanity. Your trash bin is usually filled to the top with empty, mini potato chip bags and crumpled up notebook paper." She laughs. "And the only time it ever smells this good is when you have sprayed something to cover up the scent of your piled-up gym clothes." We both chuckle.

"So, are you up for some milkshakes, burgers, and fries at Shortstop? It is your favorite." Juliana tries to persuade me to go out with puppy dog eyes and a devilish grin. I'm tired, but I decide that I would like to get out and spend some time with Julianna.

When we arrive at the pub, the hostess takes us to a booth beside an electric fireplace, the entire room is lit up with fairy lights, and the walls are filled with eccentric art. We both order virgin strawberry daiquiris with extra whipped cream. When I take a huge sip of mine, I get an immediate brain freeze and wonder why I didn't choose to order some hot chocolate with whipped cream and marshmallows. As I sit there, diagonally across from the bar, I notice a man wearing a black hat who looks familiar in some way. He's sitting alone, drinking a beer poured from the tap.

"C'mon, let's go pick out a song from the juke box!" Julianna rose from her seat, grabs my arm, and leads me to an old school juke box to find a song. I go along with her, keeping a side eye on the man I find strangely familiar. While I am focused on this individual, my pelvis bumps up against the corner of a pool table I didn't notice was in front of me.

"Are you okay?" Julianna turns around and asks. Then her eyes follow the direction of mine. "What are you staring at? Is it the bartender? Because if you don't remember we used to always come in here together and gossip about how sexy he is. That's Ben." At first, I am lost in my visual encounter. Then Julianna waves her hand in front of my face.

"What?" I ask. "Oh, yeah. It's just been so long since I've seen Ben, I just couldn't help myself." I rub the pain in my pelvis. "Ooooh, that really hurt. I forgot this pool table was here."

"*Haha.* That's okay. C'mon, let's get back to picking out some music."

Julianna scrolls through the music selection, and then proceeds to choosing a song called Californication by the Red-Hot Chili Peppers. She insists on us dancing together, and I go along with it, but for some reason I can't stop looking at this man. I only have a side angle view of him with his dark brown and gray beard and long tan leather jacket. He takes a long swig of what is left of his beer. Californication is coming to its closing melody, and I watch as the man reaches into his side pocket, pulls his black hat down over his face, and whips out a handgun, aiming it at the bartenders. The restaurant goes silent except for the dropping of bodies to the floor and the sound of chairs screeching against the floor. Julianna and I rush underneath the nearest table, and I take hold of her hand, squeezing it tightly. Julianna is struggling to breathe, and her eyes are shut tightly together. The room doesn't feel as bright any more, and the man is moving from side to side, pointing his gun nervously, threatening that if anybody moves, he will certainly shoot. The bartenders are standing still with both arms in the air.

Just then, another slim man enters the restaurant from the main door with a black beanie mask covering over his face with just enough holes for his eyes and mouth.

"Everyone, hand me all of your money and jewelry!" Nobody moves. "You heard me! I want all the money in the cash register!" The people in the room are still reluctant to move.

"Now! Now!" he demands. Everyone starts hustling in their wallets and removing their jewelry. I yank out the wallet from my purse and the $40 my mom gave me. It was a quick decision to come out with Julianna post being in the hospital and in a coma for two months, so I did not have time to scramble through my jewelry box before we left.

"Julianna," I whisper, "we have to give the men our money. You must remove your necklace and earrings and that watch you are wearing." My quiet voice is trembling. Julianna still has her eyes wrinkled shut and her fists pressed against her ears. I carefully reach behind her neck and remove her necklace. Next, I carefully remove her earrings and watch as she sits still in the same position. When I rise from under the table I turn around and my face meets the chest of the bearded man that was sitting at the bar. He grabs the cash and jewelry from my hands and moves onto the next couple lying on their bellies with their cash and jewelry in a neat pile in front of them. The bearded guy picks up their pile and moves along, but the skinny guy shifts his eyes right to sapphire and diamond set on yellow gold ring on the woman's finger. Oh no, I have a feeling this could get ugly.

The masked man walked toward the woman. The couple laid

there with their heads facing down. Aware that the armed robber was walking toward them, they refused to look up. I squint my eyes shut and wrap my arms around Julianna who was probably stuck in a deep dissociative state. He bends down above the woman's head. She's breathing heavily but trying to stay silent. He lifts her head up by her dark hair in a ponytail, exposing her face soaked in tears.

"Hand over the ring or I'll cut your finger off!" he shouts in her face.

"My mother gave me this ring," she cries, then she sobs into her hands.

"Look at me! Look at me! Does it look like a give a shit who gave you this ring. I just gave you the ultimatum. You either hand over the ring or I cut your precious finger off. So, which one is it?" He glances at the man on the floor next to her and then back at the woman's sobbing face.

"Hey, we have enough jewelry already," his partner protests. He stiffens, aware of the tension under the demanding guy's mask. The guy quietly stands up, removes the woman's ponytail from his grasp. He creeps over to the big, bearded man and becomes face to face with his masked reflection.

"Did you just say we have enough jewelry?" His tone is unpleasant and raspy. He begins to whisper, and the two break out into a whispering argument. "Listen, we aren't really bad guys if we let someone off the hook. We are taking the ring or the finger with the ring attached."

"I don't know if it's worth it."

"Well, I think it is worth it."

"What's more important, being the bad guys, or getting the money for the publishing company?"

"Both are equally important."

"We both worked hard on this book, I think we should just take what we have and get out of here. It's more than enough."

"What do you know about what is more than enough? You're still living with your mom, and you can't even get enough donuts." The skinny guy points his index and middle finger, pressing them against the chest of the bearded guy, giving him a subtle push.

While the two men squabble in their silent argument, I hear a loud thud as someone falls to the ground on the other side of the juke box, in a spot that I can't quite see. I hear the sound of an object sliding across the floor. It stops just inches away from me. It's a handgun! It looks like the Glock 19 Jared showed me when he was a lawyer! The two men suddenly stop arguing. The room is eerily silent again, and I feel the walls closing in. It feels like the lighting has dimmed, and my heart has shifted to a loud thump that could be heard from the craters of the moon.

I reach out and place my hand on the dangerous piece of metal. I curl my fingers around the gun's grip with my index finger extended, careful not to place it on the trigger. The safety is off. The only reason I know that is because Jared wanted the safety on before tossing the previous gun into the water. I notice there are no more whispering altercations, and I watch the leather boots on the men move toward me. I try to make a rapid leap out from under the table, but as I lift myself up, I bang my head hard on hard wood at the corner of the surface.

One of the guys grabs me from behind as a stumble, almost dropping to the floor, but lifting myself up from my knees. He places both hands over mine, holding them firmly as I hold the grip of the gun tightly. His friend joins the fight, and I force my finger on the trigger, press it tightly, and shoot at the bearded guy. The skinny guy releases his hold on me, and I shoot him in the leg. He fires an aimless shot, and it hits Julianna in her upper arm from under the booth. Before I can think to go help her, or to do anything in that moment, my mind shifts to me in the attic of my house living with my dad, staring at his rifle he had locked away, and he thought I didn't know the combination too. All I had to do was wait until he was out in the field behind our house chopping wood for a campfire so he could reward me with smores for complying with his psychological abuse. I could have fired at him right from my bedroom window. I would always pull the rope to the ceiling and make my way up to the attic, unlock the safe and stare at it. Knowing the option was there would always comfort me.

The big, bearded guy runs toward me again and I shoot him in the mid-chest area and watch him shiver, release his gun from his hand and fall to the ground, gasping for breath and coughing up blood simultaneously.

Suddenly, the room fills with flashing blue and red lights reflecting off the walls and the wine glasses hung above the bar. The customers are still on the floor, eyes and ears covered. The bearded guy is still struggling to breathe, and blood is still gushing from his mouth. He's lying in a pool of blood fighting for his life. The skinny guy tries to shoot at me, but his gun is empty, bullet less. He limps toward a stool and tries to keep the blood from overflowing into his jeans with his other hand. He removes his mask. It's my dad. He's not dead. I shot him, but he's still very much alive. The police barge in. I'm standing still, gun in my hand, right where the cops can see me. Right in the middle of the restaurant. I feel like I'm on a dark stage, and the spotlight is on me. I'm holding a Glock 19 handgun, and I shot two men. One whose lifeline is about to end.

When the police enter, they remove the bearded guy's mask,

it's the food truck guy who helped me escape prison! He didn't know that he helped me escape prison, but I appreciate it the same. How did he end up here, stealing money with my dad? What if I brought him here and brought my mom back to life?

Before I could find out whether he survived my blow to the chest, two officers cuff me and another two cuff my dad. They pull me out with lightning speed.

"Wait! Is that man okay? I need to find out if Julianna is okay! Please, my best friend is in there and she got shot! She needs help!" The officers ignore me and escort me to the backseat of a police car. They don't even make eye contact with me or explain my rights, they just shove me into the car. The sound of the police sirens has dissolved, replaced by the deafening sound of the ambulance coming toward Short Stop. I am relieved that a medical team is here for Juliana and the food truck guy, but no one will answer my questions regarding their well-being. *Are they going to be okay?*

The other officers throw my dad into the backseat of the driver side door. He's sweaty, but he's been given gauze for his wound, his jeans are still drenched in his DNA. There are metal jail cell bars in the middle, separating us.

"You don't understand, I just needed to make a few bucks. I didn't even kill anyone. Teenage Finlay Donovan wannabe over here was jumping the gun on everyone. You saw how scared they all were. Down on the floor like they're in the middle of a terrorist attack."

"Tell it to the judge," the driving officer responds.

"Look, I needed money for my book. You don't understand. My partner, Thomas and I are writing a children's book. I am doing the writing and Thomas is doing the illustrations. Now the last few illustrations won't be completed because of this depressed, probably bullied teen taking her anger out on innocent people in a restaurant." He turns his head directly at me. I shift my focus, avoiding eye contact. "Shouldn't you be shooting up a high school or something? Isn't that where the real enemies of your pain solicit?"

"That's enough!" the officers reply in unison. Sure, they are at least replying to him.

"But you really don't understand Sammy the Squirrel finally found the magical acorn! This is a highlighting moment in the world of children's literature!"

"A ground-breaking moment in the world of children's literature," an officer chimes in.

"What?"

"It sounds better if you say, a ground-breaking moment."

"*Hmm*. A groundbreaking moment in the world of children's literature. Well, I suppose that does sound better. Thanks!"

I feel undesirably nauseous. I bend a little forward to send some blood to my upper region. The trees keep blurring by at a rapid pace in my peripheral vision, and it's only amplifying the nausea.

"Why didn't you publish with Cliff Hanger Publishing? I'm also writing a story, and they don't charge as much as some of the other publishing companies," an officer responds.

"*Haha*, you publish with Cliff Hanger? Every author knows that they are desperate to get clients to create for them. They accept everyone." He breaks out into uncontrollable laughter. The type you get when you feel like you are going to pee your pants, your abdomen muscles are tense and slightly in pain, but the feeling is so euphoric that you're grateful that you can't stop. "You must have…" He's trying to catch his breath and discontinue laughing so that he can finish his sentence. "You

must have been rejected by all the other publishing companies!" I give him a sideways glance. It's like he has forgotten the situation at hand and that he's in trouble. His face is red, and mouth is a wide-open smile, and you can barely see his eyes, just the crow's feet and a small tear falling from the edge, a joyful tear. The officer is about to protest before his partner cuts in.
"Like I just said, tell it to the judge. Rodney don't even respond to him, it's not worth it."

*

After we drop off my dad at the police station where he will be spending the night, the officers proceed to explain that I will be taken to a juvenile detention center.

"We are unsure what is going to happen with you. We will bring you to stay with the other delinquents and then the judge will decide whether you stay and whether you can be returned to your mother. Clearly, she is struggling to raise an adolescent. I'm sure the judge will provide her with some resourceful information on how she can get the help that she needs. You may be sent to a group home or a foster family after that."

This is awful, I only spent one hour with my mom since I returned from the hospital. It's unclear if I will ever see her again! I struggle to swallow as there is no saliva left in my mouth and my throat is completely dry. "It is well-known that delinquency in adolescence is a direct result of poor parenting. When a parent is psychologically controlling, teens just want to lash out and go out of control, sometimes on killing sprees to unleash their anger and frustration." He makes a fist in the air with his right hand. "The best technique is behavioral control, giving rewards when a child possesses positive qualities like autonomous, socially accepted behavior." He smiles.

Thomas turns to him, passing him a weirded-out stare. "You read way too much *Psychology Today*. Besides, we are talking about a girl who has been in this world for fifteen years. She's been in school. She hasn't been isolated from the outside world. She should already have a good sense of what is right and wrong. It is her responsibility to display positive behaviors. Not go out with a gun shooting everyone. Besides, her mom could be working really hard all day to support her only child. This is how she repays her? Destroying her reputation?"

"Destroying her reputation? No, no, no. It's the mom's responsibility. Plus, we don't even know the whole story."

"A good amount of time in juvie will teach her all she needs to know. She deserves to know the consequences of her own poor behavior."

"All right, all right. Let's just drop it right there. We could be going around in circles like this forever."

"Okay, but it's her responsibility." Rodney looks over with a raging sneer. "What?"

"She has daddy issues! She doesn't even have a father!"

"We don't even know for a fact that she doesn't have a father." The two weirdos interrupt their argument to glance back at me. "Do you have a father?" Well, the other dude that was just in the car is my father, but I don't think he actually is right now.

"No."

"See, daddy issues, she doesn't have a father." The car goes silent again.

My eyes catch Rodney's eyes in the rearview mirror. "Oh no, don't give me those sad puppy dog eyes. Thomas, she's giving me the sad puppy dog eyes." Thomas turns around in the passenger seat to look at me.

"Look, kid, we don't make up the law, and we don't get to decide what happens to you. You clearly have some unresolved issues. You're only a teen and you've already shot two people. The only responsibility we have is to enforce the law. Maybe you can share your story with the other delinquents in juvie, and they will comfort you and help you through this difficult time."

"Ugh, Thomas, we don't know what juvie is like for teens. We only know what it's like to drop them off there. Don't fill her head with empty promises. It could be the worst time of her life." I begin to sob, with my chin pressed against my neck. "Oh God, I've done it again." Jerry shifts the rearview mirror so he can't see my reflection.

The car is noiseless as I press my forehead against the bars separating me from the glass of the window. Lines on the road and trees blur by as I try to find what I am feeling in the mist of this moment preceding my impending fate.

The police vehicle skids to a halt as dead crows or ravens start falling from the sky at a rapid pace. A bunch of them land roughly on the windshield, cracking the glass and inhibiting the car from continuing its path. The officer pulls over and reaches for his walkie talky thing to reach out to dispatch. A lifeless black bird crashes into my window, pressing against a piece of notebook paper with the words ***Run away with me*** clearly written upon it. The bird slips down the car window leaving a trail of blood as it falls to the ground.

"Thomas to dispatch, can you hear me. We have a 10-91 here. It seems a bunch of...1qa." He takes another peek out the window, he squints as if that will assist in figuring out what is going on. "There seem to be some ravens or crows or whatever that have died and are falling from the sky. Hello? Officer Jerry to dispatch."

"Dispatch probably thinks this is some sort of joke." Rodney pulls the walkie-talkie from his partner's hands.

"Rodney to dispatch. THIS IS NOT A JOKE! Our windshield is cracked with dead birds and blood everywhere. We are in the middle of transporting a delinquent teen who shot up Short Stop Sports Bar. Is anyone there? Can you hear me?"

IT IS OVER… FOR NOW!